At the Upper Villa Tyde

Ophelia Finsen

Also by Ophelia Finsen:

Lovers of Old Films
This is Living
Society of Lost Causes
The Women of Jimanac
Skye
The Romanian

ISBN: 978-0-9559923-8-4

PART ONE

She found the bag of postcards by the sink after throwing up in the station toilets.

It was a struggle getting in and out of the cubicle, lumbering suitcases and bags as if she was rather indiscreetly smuggling a body out for disposal. The station tannoy announcement reminded passengers to keep their possessions within sight at all times. Undeclared items would be removed from human contact and destroyed in a manner seen fit by the authorities. So in went the suitcase, the rucksack and the overstuffed handbag. Barely any space for a girl to lean over a toilet bowl and convulse up her nerves. Pulling the last piece of toilet paper out of the dispenser, she wiped her mouth, stains of peach lipstick smeared on the off-white. Who got dressed up for a seven hour train journey? She'd spent an hour getting ready this morning, which was not normal, even for parties. Careful makeup, long dark hair blown dry in curlers then arranged in an up-do that was ready for the red carpet, not stuffy train carriages. This was not standard behaviour. Certainly not for someone who looked as though they were permanently leaving home.

She was aware of the bag the moment she staggered out of the toilet cubicle. A strap on her rucksack caught on the door handle, jolting her in a momentary pause. She swore, tugging the rucksack free and stumbling to the sinks. Washed her hands, looking at the bag from the corner of her eye. What if it had a bomb in it? She was the only person in the ladies toilets, and weren't abandoned bags and packages meant to be treated with the upmost suspicion these days? Although Shrewsbury train station, central-west England, didn't feel like the most obvious of terrorist targets.

Drying her hands, she gave the line of toilet cubicles another check to be sure she was the only person in the room. Side stepping, she approached the bag. It was a thick paper bag with twisted paper handles, the kind you expected from shops that wanted to look a little more upmarket, or a little more eco-friendly. She hadn't heard of the branding printed on the side of the bag. A finger curling over the edge and she pulled the side down and towards herself, looking in to the contents.

Postcards. Seemingly hundreds of postcards. Her brow knitted, and she stepped unabashed up to the bag, any pretence of hiding curiosity forgotten. She picked up the first postcard, a sunset image, overtly-orange and bleached as if it had been left out too long in the very sun it depicted. Curled at the corners. She turned it over. It had been sent from Trinidad and Tobago, over ten years ago. The message was written in curling, dramatic script. Sent to Wales. Another postcard, pulled at random. A view of Berlin...

"The 15:27 Arriva Trains Wales service from Birmingham International to Aberystwyth and Pwlheli is now approaching platform four."

She looked up from the postcard in a panic as the platform announcement blared out. Her train already arriving? Surely not, she'd had over half an hour to wait at Shrewsbury, knew she could loiter. But the announcement had been clear, and on checking her watch, she saw time had gone quickly. This was her train, and she couldn't miss it. Certainly she could get on the next one, her ticket allowed it, but this third and final stage of the journey was over three hours and she didn't want to delay. She'd set off from York station ten minutes to twelve, travelled across to Manchester with all the holiday makers and jetsetters, hopping off at Manchester Piccadilly and sprinting to catch the train to Shrewsbury. She had to get herself and her weighty luggage onto platform four now.

But. Her eyes lingered on the bag of postcards. She'd only looked at a couple, but she got the impression every card had been individually written and sent from a multitude of places. These were keepsakes, the markers of strangers' lives – the senders and the receivers. It was, to be frank, none of her business. Whoever had left this would probably want them back, would register the empty feeling in their hand and come rushing back to the toilets after a heart-stopping moment, thinking back through the course of the day. Where are my mementos? She should have left well alone, and usually she was ever so good, suffering from a particularly acute sense of guilt and world conscience. Today the devil was on her shoulder and she wanted to read these mysterious postcards, delve into a story and a past she knew nothing about.

She didn't have time to stand and mentally debate the moral aspects of the scenario. Pushing her hand right through the straps of her handbag, so that it hung weighty in the crook of her elbow, she took the postcard bag in one hand, the handle of her pull-along suitcase in the other and ran out to platform four.

A local train, only three carriages long, pulled up to the platform, rolling to a neat stop. A hiss as the doors opened, passengers relieved to get out of the carriages and into fresh air. It was a particularly warm day. There were only a handful waiting to get on at her carriage, but having arrived late, she was the last to get on, struggling with all of her baggage.

Shoving her suitcase into a lower luggage rack by the doors with a final kick, she staggered down the central aisle to her reserved seat, grateful to see that she didn't have a neighbour reserved in the aisle seat beside her. Unceremoniously dropping her handbag and illicitly gained postcard collection onto the empty seat, she shrugged off her rucksack, feeling like a weak body builder trying to lift too great a weight as she pushed it into the overhead luggage rack. She collapsed into the seat beside the window, her head resting against the glass. Final train to catch. Watching the passengers, part way through journeys, travel just starting, or perhaps ending, walking along the platform. She twisted, catching sight of the bag of postcards, and guiltily put them on the floor under her seat. Wouldn't it be awful if the true owner was on this train as well, and in walking by to locate their own seat, noticed their personal treasures, tragically misplaced in a moment of absent-mindedness, sitting by a stranger on a train? How to explain that one?

A voice on the internal speaker system welcomed passengers aboard, in Welsh. She did not understand a word until the woman began to list the places the train would be stopping at before reaching its final destination at Aberystwyth. It certainly was a local train; there would be a total of twenty-five stops before the train reached her destination of Porthmadog; and from there it would continue on through north Wales.

She closed her eyes and pressed her forehead to the grimy, cool glass window. She would be glad when she got where she was going.

Stop Three: Caersws. Quarter past four: the train at the little station in the middle of nowhere. Everything was in quaint miniature; the station looked like a country cottage against a brief platform. Although it was not as small as one she'd seen on the way through the hills; a request stop that was literally a platform and nothing more. The mist had been rolling down the peaks, blotting out the colour of the sky. Duller, duller and duller. By the time the train reached Caersws – still not at the coast where the long journey of many stops would begin – there was an announcement, first in Welsh, then English, informing passengers that there was a problem with the train and they'd all have to disembark. The lights weren't working and they would have to get onto a different train to complete the journey. As the train would be separating at Machynlleth, passengers on the long stretch up to Pwllheli (this included her) were reminded to get on either coach A or B. Passengers to Aberystwyth should stay in coach C.

Struggling back into her rucksack; handbag and postcard bag in hands, Beryl ungainly tottered down the aisle, taking her suitcase at the door, and hurried on to the next train. Another delay, to lengthen the journey. Perhaps if the sun had been shining, the route along the coast would have been enjoyable. But it rained; the sea mist thickened and there was little to look at other than the raindrops racing horizontally over the exterior of the glass. Her body thumping with the steady ta-ta over every join of ironwork railway.

They arrived in Porthmadog, a little coastal town in north Wales, at seven in the evening, about fifteen minutes late. A thin trickle of passengers alighted, she being one of the last due to her luggage. Not even attempting to carry her belongings in any dignified manner, Beryl dropped her rucksack and bags ungraciously on the platform in the drizzle and tried to collect herself.

It was a small station, looking to be unmanned. On this side there weren't even any buildings, the other platform boasting a small building would be the platform to wait on for the return journey. A short set of steps into a car park, then the grey-washed spread of Porthmadog ahead. Most people appeared to be met, friends and relatives greeting each other in Welsh, a language so far from English, so bizarre to her ears, that she felt like a stranger in a foreign country. She should have really made arrangements for when she got here, but she noted there was a couple of taxis idling at the side of the car park, and thanked whatever higher being was responsible for her good fortune.

The driver's door to the first taxi opened as she struggled down the steps to the car park. A tall Welshman with a generous stomach, grey-to-white slicked hair and at least one gold ring on each hand, walked forward and said something to her in Welsh.

"Sorry?"

"Ah, English," he nodded, almost pityingly that she was presumably only mono-lingual. It was not meant unkindly. "I was asking if you'll be wanting a taxi. Not really the evening for walking to your digs, and if it's your first time here, you might not know where you're going." The sing-song of his accent sounded oddly cheerful against the general atmosphere. A native defence long built over generations to keep positive thinking up against the rain that a green Wales needed to keep it green, but the locals sick of the weather.

"Yes, thank you." She let him take the suitcase, but was careful to keep the postcard bag out of the way of helpful hands. "I've been given this address," she added, pulling out a scribbled note from a side pocket of her bursting handbag.

He took the piece of paper. "Castle Deudraeth," he read out, pronouncing it Dye-drath and making her thankful she had just given him the address rather than attempting to say the name. "Why, you could have got off at Minfford, a stop back."

"Really?"

"Not to worry, I can drive you over there. It's not much further. We'll soon be over the cob."

She put her rucksack into the boot of the car, but kept handbag and postcards with her as she got into the backseat. The taxi driver climbed into the car. Final stage of the journey. "Away to Portmeirion for a holiday then?" he asked conversationally as he pulled out of the car park.

"Yes," she started a little uncertainly, not wishing to explain exactly how long for fear he may come to the wrong conclusions. "Well, they gave me the address of the castle. I don't think that's part of the village, is it?"

"No, it's just outside, but it's part of the estate. Of course, they make everyone check in there, even if they're staying in one of the cottages. But I suppose with you on your own, you'll be in a room at the castle. Or maybe at the hotel in the village."

"I'm not sure." There had been mention of a home from home, but it all seemed very vague now locals were asking for specifics.

He laughed. "You're not sure? This booked on a whim?"

"It was a present."

"A present! Very nice. A weekend away here. Better than another pair of socks any day of the week."

Castle Deudraeth, stood at the end of a longish drive, looked like a large manor house wanting oh so badly to be a proper castle ready for war. It was vaguely familiar, she remembered it had been used as the exterior shot for a hospital in an old sixties television series. Crenulations across the top of every block section of the property; a slim, rounded tower at one end, and an entrance way sticking out at the front like a mini keep. Ivy engulfed the front of the building, leaves pouring droplets of rainwater down to the earth.

Having paid the taxi driver, she paused at the entrance to the hotel, looking at the drizzle, the dark grey skies and the car retreating back down the road. It had been a long day. Time to go in.

There was a solitary man in a neatly pressed suit at the reception desk. Brass buttons on the jacket made him look like a grown-up cross between a bellboy and a soldier. "Good evening," he greeted her in the distinctive accent of North Wales. "Will you be staying with us?" he asked, somewhat rhetorically, glancing over her baggage. "Do you have a reservation?"

"Yes."

"Can I take your name please?"

"Beryl Sinise."

"Beryl," he repeated, the name almost put as an accusatory question as if she was already lying. People these days weren't called Beryl, particularly girls who didn't look as though they'd even hit thirty yet. To be fair, most people took on some kind of bemused look on hearing her name, because it was ridiculous. It had been her ball and chain throughout her teenage years. Her mother was the kind of person who didn't like to run with the flow, and felt a need to use the name to preserve it for posterity's sake. At twenty-five, she was used to it well enough, but growing accustomed had taken some time.

"I don't seem to be finding your name…"

A slight moment of panic. "Maybe it's under my aunt's name. She booked it. Portia Montague."

"Portia Montague," he repeated slowly. Another overblown name. It sounded like a range of flowery blouses for rich maiden aunts and ladies of a certain age to wear out to lunch. Not an aunt's name. Perhaps this woman claiming to be called Beryl was just deluded and wandering. "I can't find her here. You're sure you're booked into Castle Deudraeth?"

"I'm just assuming. She said I'd be staying at Portmeirion."

"I wonder if you're in the hotel," he muttered, typing something else into the computer. A click, then he stopped, raised his eyebrows and pursed his lips, as if to suggest what he had found had not been expected. "I've found you," he declared. "You're booked into the Upper Tyde, already paid for by your aunt it appears..." A pause, scrolling through the information. "And it's a block booking for three months." He looked up sharply at her. She hadn't screamed upper class money at him when she'd entered the hotel, with her rucksack fit to bursting, a standard pull-along suitcase and handbag. And then that rain-drop stained paper carrier she had. "I think you're going to have a very enjoyable stay here. I'll just get your keys."

He turned and paused at a notice board of hanging keys, hand hovering before selecting the correct ones.

"What's the Upper Tyde?" Beryl asked as she took the keys from him.

"It's the Villa Tyde. A property in the village. It's been split into two separate self-catering flats. You're on the first floor. There's parking to the rear of the property. I can get you a permit for your windscreen."

"I don't need one; I came here on the train."

"Oh." His eyes flicked to the window, where the rain had grown decidedly heavier. He could hardly send her out in that with all her luggage and one of the tourist maps flapping in the wind to try and find her new summer home. "I'll go find someone to drive you down there."

Beryl woke up early the next day. It took some time to remember where she was, or even why. Lying on her back, gazing up at the white ceiling, she could have sworn she'd seen the movement of light as though she was beside a great body of water. Ripples playing over the paintwork.

The light coming through the bedroom window wasn't particularly strong yet. Her eyes hung on the details of the room. It was a tidy space, carefully arranged and with neutral white walls. Comfortable but void of any personal touches. The self catering flat, a home from home for the next three months. As soon as she'd found out about the booking, a revelation that had been accidentally well-timed with other issues in her life, she'd made plans to flee to Wales, getting train tickets ready to arrive the first day of the booking. There had only been a week to wait, then she escaped her everyday life, the job that was grinding her down and a flatmate she'd grown out of.

Dressed in a cotton nightdress, looking more like a strappy pinafore dress than night attire, she got up and walked through the flat to the living room. There was a glass panelled door which opened out onto a small terrace balcony. Through the trees there was a view down onto the centre of the village, with the formal garden area, shallow pool, beds of brightly coloured annuals, and Balinese dancers perched on tall columns. It was bright, fantastical, exotic, and a series of explosions of colour and features. The buildings surrounding the garden area were painted in bold yellows, pinks and blues. The architecture was very Italian in style, and gave the place a story book atmosphere. She'd never been to Portmeirion before, although she'd seen pictures on the television, and from the sixties television series, *The Prisoner*, in which it looked as though the village had been purpose-built for the story concept, although that certainly wasn't the case.

She watched a figure in jeans and a shapeless T-shirt trundle a wheelbarrow up the side of a small cottage, setting it down just in front the water pool. Beryl's stomach rumbled – she hadn't eaten anything yesterday evening, instead going straight to bed. And she already knew there wouldn't be anything in the little kitchen she'd briefly glanced over. She'd have to go into the village and see if there was anywhere to eat. Although as the village itself was a tourist attraction rather than a permanent community, she didn't expect to find any of the regular village features – no pub, no local shop, other than the type selling postcards and souvenirs.

Leaving the balcony, she returned to the double bedroom – one of two bedrooms in the flat – and quickly changed. Glanced at herself in the mirror and paused out of vanity's sake. Her carefully styled hair of yesterday was scruffy, falling out of place, but still in some semblance of a style, the old hairspray trying to keep its shape. She took a red headscarf out of her suitcase and tied it around her head like a wide headband, covering over the worst. A flick of mascara and she was in her sandals, scuttling out of the door and down the steps to ground level.

The village was quiet, virtually empty at this time in the morning. A tourist attraction in itself, it wasn't yet open to the general public. Guests staying on site at the hotel by the sea front were just waking up; self-catering residents slumbering in their temporary homes. At the bottom of the steps she landed around the back of the Villa Tyde building where she was staying. Following a path down in-between two buildings – the Chantry of fine red pan tiles, and Chantry Row, a terrace of brightly painted houses with neat balconies out front – she took a stepped path down a short steep route onto a single track tarmac road. A little way along this, there were wide curved steps down into the formal garden area she had seen from her balcony window. Heading diagonally out across the grass, she walked in the general direction of an idyllic small white-walled cottage with blue trim. The wheelbarrow was still parked beside it, the figure in jeans and a shapeless sweater leant over the receptacle cutting lengths of green string.

Hearing footsteps, the figure twisted up to look. A woman, at first glance with the look of a hippie, ash blonde hair loosely tied up and a shaggy, slightly stoned demeanour. She had a short, rather compact face with a distinctly broad smile, brows naturally lowered. A skinny frame that was somehow disguised and accentuated simultaneously by the shapeless clothes. She dropped the ball of twine and nodded to Beryl. "*Bore da.*" She smiled, an open, easy smile. "*Ydych chi yma i weithio yn y shop?*"

Beryl felt self conscious about the fact that she didn't speak Welsh. An ignorant intruder. She started to shake her head, wondering for a stupid moment if there were Welsh speakers who didn't speak English.

The woman seemed to take her body language for a reply. She looked a little concerned. Or was it confusion. "*Ydych chi eisiau help?*"

Beryl had reached her, stepping off the lawn and onto an area of tarmac. "I'm sorry," she started. "I don't speak Welsh. Do you..." she left the question hanging – she couldn't ask the woman if she spoke English. It seemed too silly a question.

The woman's mouth formed a small 'o' and she nodded her understanding. Then grinned again. "I see. Not to worry. Although I think you've answered my question by not answering it."

"What were you asking?"

"There's a new girl supposed to be starting in the bookshop today. I thought you might be her."

"No, I'm not. Although how do you know?"

"You'd need to speak Welsh. You need to speak Welsh for a lot of the posts here. Although you could probably get a casual summer job in the gardens with just English." She broke out into a healthy laugh. "I don't suppose you're here for work. You must be a paying guest. You staying down at the hotel?"

Beryl shook her head. "One of the flats. I just got here last night. I don't have any food in. I don't suppose there's anywhere to buy anything?"

The woman shook her head. "Just the prepared kind. But the supermarket in Porthmadog delivers – you should order on line." She paused, taking the conversation as an excuse for a break. She took a small plastic bag of tobacco out of her jeans pocket and started to roll up a cigarette. "But that's not going to help you right now."

"I should be able to get something at the hotel."

"Bit early. They won't be serving yet. You do know what time it is?" She offered her the tobacco pouch as if Beryl might want to roll her own. Beryl declined. "It's the crack of dawn and it's just us gardeners out and about." She put the tobacco pouch away, and holding the thin, crooked cigarette in the corner of her mouth, she put a foot forward, offering her hand. "I'm Cerys by the way."

"Beryl."

"Beryl?" Cerys made her name sound more musical than it usually was. "I've not met a Beryl your age before."

"That's what most people tell me." Beryl wasn't sure how old Cerys was. Anywhere between early twenties to forties wouldn't have surprised her. She had a bronzed, slightly weathered look, wind-twisted hair and a natural beauty that was quite proud of the fact Cerys did very little fussing over her appearance.

"You should keep that," Cerys said, tapping her right temple as if this would be a clue to a riddle later on. She lit her cigarette and exhaled smoke, taking the object away from her mouth. "These little unique features are what make us special." She glanced at her watch, then picked up the secateurs from the wheelbarrow and put them in the pouch on her sweatshirt. "Brew time," she announced, "Come with me, meet the crew. We'll make sure you don't starve."

"I wouldn't want to..."

"Not a problem," Cerys assured her, sauntering with an easy gait over to the grass. "Come and see behind the scenes. You staying here long?"

"Three months."

"Three months!" Cerys almost swallowed her cigarette. "There's a story there. If you're going to be here that long, I'm sure you'll have time to tell it sometime."

Beryl followed Cerys, back up the path she had just come down between the two fine houses, past her own new home and up the road towards the main entrance – gatehouses and workshops included. Following a path around the back of a pottery workshop – not up and running yet today, they came to a door out of which sing-song merry-sounding Welsh conversation flowed and the smell of coffee and bacon frying wafted.

Cerys marched boldly through the doorway, Beryl following awkwardly in the Welsh woman's shadow. She didn't really belong in the staff area, and very obviously a masculine environment, she noted as her eyes darted through the interior of the room. She and Cerys were the first women of the morning to enter the room, probably would be for the entire day.

Conversation fizzled out and eyes immediately went to the stranger, trying to work out if she was local, perhaps the new girl to work in the bookshop, or some other undisclosed newcomer. But their curiosity was not as much as their surprise when Cerys announced loudly "Good Morning boys!" The loud brash cheerfulness was enough to raise most eyebrows at this early hour in the morning; but even more shocking was the lack of a *Bore Da*, and instead a formal English Good Morning.

A slightly rounded man with a face like sunshine, shaggy orange hair like dropping leaves off the top of a strawberry, turned around to look at Cerys. "There's no need for English at this time of the morning. And anyway, haven't you heard, it's no smoking in the work place."

Cerys grinned, the cigarette barely balancing between her lips which squeezed together in a pout. She puffed smoke like a dragon, then caught the butt end of the cigarette between two fingers just before it dropped from her mouth. She walked over to the draining board beside the sunshine man, and stubbed out the glowing embers. "Dafydd, this is Beryl. Beryl, Dafydd," she introduced them. "Dafydd is our under under gardener."

Dafydd spluttered into his tea. "Putting me in my place. So Beryl, are you the new girl?"

"No, I don't work here."

"Really? I like your headscarf."

"She's going to be living in the village for a while."

"Ah, paying guest."

"English?"

Beryl wasn't sure who had asked. "Yes, I..." She looked through the room, her gazed falling on a small table with red and white checked wax table top. Two older, gruff looking men sat looking at her, but as soon as she met their gaze, they abruptly looked back at one another and pointedly continued their conversation in Welsh.

"Don't mind them, they're grumpy old farts," Dafydd confided. "So what are you doing hanging around the gardeners' staff room at this time of the morning?"

"Found her walking around with a rumbling stomach," Cerys said.

"Hunger, is it?" Dafydd boomed. "I'm just frying up a bit of bacon. Do you want a bacon butty?"

"I don't eat meat. But you don't need to go to any..."

"English *and* a vegetarian," Dafydd joked. "You've not got much going for you, have you? But I do like your headscarf."

"Ignore them," Cerys advised as she headed for the kettle to make tea. "They mean no harm. And there's nothing wrong with being a vegetarian. I happen to be vegan."

"So how long have you been here?" Dafydd asked.

"I just arrived last night."

"Not long then. How are you finding it? All a bit strange? Can't understand a word?"

"She could always learn Welsh whilst she's here," Cerys jumped back into the conversation, the tinkle of a teaspoon against the side of a mug as she spun a teabag around in the hot water. "Kev's learning, you know."

Dafydd laughed. "Yeah, but learning what?" He leaned over to Beryl conspiratorially. "Kev's a Liverpudlian and one of the few people to get a job in the village and not speak a word of the lingo. He scrubs pots down at the hotel. Cerys is determined that everyone should learn Welsh."

"I really don't understand why they don't get the chance in English and Scottish schools," Cerys commented, passing Beryl a mug of milky tea. "We're all one united kingdom. We should learn about the different cultures and languages."

"Half the bloody Welsh don't speak Welsh. Why would the English want to learn?"

"That's fine talk coming from a Welshman."

"Good day!"

The trio by the sink stopped and looked to the open door. A small man in jeans and a T-shirt advertising a rock concert grinned back in at the collection. He sauntered into the room, immediately homing in on Beryl. "Are you the new girl?"

"No, I don't work here."

"Beryl's staying in the village."

"Really?" the man, obviously the Liverpudlian, Kev, judging by the accent, raised his eyebrows and smiled in appreciation. "Well, I've no complaints. It's nice to have another young lady in the village."

Young lady? It sounded like something an old man might say, but he only looked about fifteen years old. Even the old men had probably dropped the phrase; the last person Beryl could remember calling her 'young lady' was her mother, when Beryl had accidentally knocked over a can of blue wall paint over the carpet in the living room. That had been a lot of years ago.

"We've just been discussing the Welsh language," Dafydd told him.

Kev looked at Beryl. "Do you speak Welsh?"

"Not a word."

"But she's going to learn," Cerys added as if this had already been decided. "How are you getting on, Kev?"

"Not bad. I was reading a book last night before I went to bed. Learned a couple of new phrases. *Rhowter hers*."

Dafydd started sniggering. Cerys sighed.

"*Mynnwych wledd i'ch arweddawdr, meibion eillion llwydion llawdr*."

Dafydd burst out loud laughing. Cerys looked disapprovingly at Kev. "Do you even understand what that means?"

"Of course, it was translated into English on the other side."

She rolled her eyes, then looked over at Beryl. "Kev's gotten hold of a book of dirty Welsh poems. Not really the kind of education I'd been intending for him."

"Don't knock it. I'm actually reading poetry now."

"Our minds still in the gutter?" A fifth man arrived to join their group, particularly tall, thin, lank, almost weightless despite his size, he had walked in unnoticed. He had a rather bony face, hooded eyelids, a large, arching nose, the kind of face caricaturists would draw with ease. He looked like a deep thinker, either that or someone who was prone to falling asleep on spec. Eyelids almost, but not quite, too heavy to hold up for long periods of time. Unkempt, dark hair, seeming too much for his head. His long, scrawny fingers reached for the tea. Beryl was relieved to note the English accent. Now there were three in the room who didn't speak the local lingo.

"Adrien," Cerys spoke to him. "You'll not have met Beryl yet."

"Beryl?" he questioned, his gaze sweeping around, almost an audible sound, and he noted Beryl's presence for the first time. "Are you the new girl?"

This was growing tiresome. "No. I'm just staying here."

"Going to be learning Welsh with me," Kev added.

She couldn't recall having shown any interest in even learning a few words, and now she was roped into lessons, taught by Cerys, classmates with Kev. Beryl wondered if she ought to have stayed in bed.

"Has Cerys persuaded you to learn Welsh?" she asked Adrien out of polite conversation.

Adrien regarded her, considered his reply for a moment. "No."

"I don't need to," Cerys expanded.

"Adrien," one of the men at the table interrupted the conversation. Something was barked in Welsh and the two men stood up, making a move to go back to work. Adrien put his mug down and said something equally incomprehensible back to them.

Cerys grinned. "He already speaks Welsh. Learned it for fun at university."

The older men left the room. Adrien gulped down his tea. "Looks like I'm back to the grindstone already. Anon, dear friends."

"Yeah, anon and toodal pip," Dafydd responded. "Now, Kev, can I interest you in a bacon butty?"

Portmeirion was not really a village. Certainly not of the meaning of a village; a sedentary community, families in cottages, parents off to work, children to school, all gathering in the evening again for a shared meal. No police station, no local doctor, no supermarket, no post office – naturally, because there were no permanent residents to service.

On the contrary side, one could not suggest that Portmeirion was an artificial village created as a theme park to lure tourists to North Wales. Such a statement could only be declared in ignorance of the village's history. Portmeirion was an artwork and architectural project exploring beauty and magic. Portmeirion counted its age in decades. The creator bought the original little fishing village on the coast of Wales in the 1920s. An abandoned wilderness on steep wooded land, rocky cliffs and a sea that would sweep forth and back, revealing great plains of sand on its departure.

Over the decades, Portmeirion, as renamed by its new owner, grew up, houses like seedlings, one after another up the steep slopes. Brightly coloured buildings, now self catering cottages and flats, lined the little road down to the seafront, where a ship was built into the seawall. Close by the hotel, white walled with blue trim, guests were served on a stylish patio. There were gardens, water features, follies and statues, an Italian style bell tower, or campanile, golden Balinese dancers on tall pedestals at corners of the central garden area, and flowers and trees bursting forth. A fairy tale village straight out of children's fables.

After breakfast and chatting, the gardeners had returned to work and Beryl was alone, back on her own side of the divide – the paying guest, but not quite, because with Beryl's job, this wasn't the kind of holiday or retreat she could have ever afforded. A day pass was the kind of girl she usually was.

She'd returned to the flat for the remainder of the morning. In the living room – a living room all of her own, no flatmate to share with – she had set out her laptop computer on the little dining table and connected to the internet. Checking which supermarkets were set up in Porthmadog, the nearest town, she'd ordered a healthy load of groceries online. She was going to be here for three months, so she might as well stock up. Her rent was paid, so there was just the food issue to worry about. There was a slot for an eight pm delivery that day, which she'd booked.

There was a lazy sweeping main road through the village, swinging down like an uncoiled snake, skirting the lines of buildings, curling around the back of the gardens like a protective arm, and unfurling at the end by the hotel at the sea front. Beryl followed this track, wandering past the day trippers. It wasn't the height of the tourist season yet, but there were already a reasonable number of visitors. She'd passed by a man in a black blazer with white trim, like a chalk line at a crime scene. He had a long purple scarf around his neck. As they'd passed, he'd flipped one end of the scarf over his shoulder and raised his eyebrows at her as if they were sharing a secret in passing. "Be seeing you."

What? Beryl slowed down and looked back. He hadn't stopped, and was swiftly marching up the hill. She didn't know him. He was behind other clusters of tourists. No matter. She turned back and continued along the road.

There was a little restaurant serving lunch at the top corner of the road. Beryl sat outside at a white painted iron table, eating macaroni cheese. The back of the outdoor eating area was lined with a rich green privet hedge. Statues, Grecian styled women with blank stares, just emerging from spaces in the thick foliage.

Further down towards the end of the road, past another garden with a round blue swimming pool reserved for guests. Set out against a green lawn, brilliant white sun loungers, like determined streaks in a painting of stark colours. She went to the hotel, walking around the front and leaning against the stone wall, looking down to the next level of walkway. The ship was directly ahead of her, at first glance just moored to the harbour, but in reality built into the wall. Crossing her arms, she leaned into the wall, gazing across the estuary. The tide was out, and there was a long expanse of wet flat sand, cut apart here and there with streams, leftovers from the sea.

"A country singer from the 50s..." someone at one of the tables on the patio area commented.

Beryl watched a seagull swoop in the sky.

"Blue gingham shirt."

The seagull landed on top of the ship.

"And a red headscarf controlling curls."

Her eyes narrowed slightly. She was being talked about, either that or talked at. She looked over to her right, to the patio where polite waiters would serve cream teas to old dears in the afternoon. A slightly overweight man with a ruddy face, unbrushed auburn hair and a dependence on the prop up the table was giving him that was really too much for this time of day, lifted a wine glass in her direction. "Cheers!"

She smiled weakly and turned away. Why was it that she always attracted the attention of the drunken losers and freaks? They probably sensed her shyness, that slightness of insecurity that work colleagues bitched was pathetic, and found an easy target, an audience that would be too polite to get up and walk away. Either that or just tell them to piss off.

The man emptied the glass, glanced over at the bottle on his table and considered an immediate refill before deciding it could wait a little. It didn't do to be legless before dinner time. He smoothed the cream lapel of his suit jacket – she'd better not think he was just some drunken sot; didn't she know who he was? He observed the way she idly leant against the wall, watching nothing in particular. She wasn't in a rush to explore Portmeirion. She was here alone.

"Day tripper or resident?"

She didn't react, perhaps a slight tensing of the shoulders, but otherwise she ignored him. She thought he was an embarrassing old drunk. Old drunk, his arse. He would only have five years on her; well, most probably ten at least, he conceded, considering his thirty-sixth birthday was approaching far too quickly. "I am still talking to you."

Beryl looked back at him.

"Day tripper or resident?"

"Sorry?"

"For goodness sake, I'm not going to bite," he sighed, raising his eyes. "I know your mother must have told you not to speak to strangers, but that was for when you were a little girl," he paused, wondering if she was still a little girl. "Let's have an exchange of information. I'll answer, then you can do the same. I'm a resident in the village; I'm staying at the hotel."

"I'm staying in the village," she admitted.

"Now we're getting somewhere." He filled his glass again. "Would you care for a drink?"

"No thank you."

"Too early? Well, we're residents on holiday." He set the bottle down. "Are you here for a weekend or the whole week?"

"Three months."

"Three months!" He was surprised by this. "Now you have caught my interest. Come and join me here and tell me about yourself. I come and stay at the hotel for long periods on a regular basis. I know about all the long-term guests."

She faltered, certain the sensible, courageous thing to do would be to walk away. But she had to admit she was interested and repulsed at the same time; odd people had that question mark shaped door she just couldn't help opening. "It's not a regular thing," she told him, "Just a one off visit."

"Not enjoying the experience so far?"

"No, I mean yes. It seems very nice here. Just a little out of my price range."

He laughed out loud. "You're renting one of the cottages for three months and this is out of your price range?"

"I'm not renting," she explained, "It's another unsuitable and inappropriate gift from my aunt." Giving up on a sense of decorum and chances of making the right kind of friends – this change in direction would end up with the same result as every other previous attempt, regardless of bold resolutions – she joined him at the little table. "She likes to give very expensive and pointless presents. It's just lucky that this came at a point in my life when I needed a break."

"Is there something you would have rather had? Are you a spoilt little rich girl?"

"Hardly. I haven't a penny to my name. Sensibly she could have just given me the money and I could have bought a car or used it to move into a nicer flat, but..." she shrugged. "Aunt Portia doesn't do sensible. When I was a student, with loans for my tuition fees and living costs, she paid for the rental of a very expensive diamond necklace and tiara..."

"How deliciously decadent."

"But there were so many things I could have better spent the money on. And as it was, I was so terrified of losing them, or having them stolen."

"But you had an experience you would have otherwise never dared squander your money on, had you even had such sums of wealth."

"Maybe. But when you're struggling to cover the basics, who cares about diamonds?"

"That's a very unfeminine thing to say." He smiled to himself as her eyes widened as if insulted. She had a very dark, innocent look, with thick black 50s style eyeliner and black lashes.

"So who are you?"

"No one special. Who are you?"

"That's a little direct. Me? Well, I suppose you've told me about Aunt Portia, so it's my turn now. The name's Noel, Noel Farthing." He extended a hand.

"Noel Farthing?" Beryl repeated as she weakly shook his hand. A coincidence she supposed. This couldn't be the famous Farthing who sat upon her bookshelf, as he did in millions of other households across the world.

"The very same. Yes, it is I; I am *the* Noel Farthing, author of *Summer in the Fishbowl*."

"You're a writer."

"That's very astute of you."

"A successful writer," she breathed.

Noel burst into a loud roar of laughter. "That's a statement that deserves the disbelief you apply to it. A successful writer. There aren't very many of those. Tell me, I'll wager you have my book at home."

"Of course." She'd perhaps not mention that she had read several times, nor that she'd brought it with her to read again during her long holiday. It was an incredibly clever book, something of an instant classic. It had been translated into some thirty languages. A debut book that had made him a household name, pages devoured by readers, but also able to cross boundaries over into literary circles. Anyone who claimed any interest in fiction, however slight, had read the Noel Farthing book. The Noel Farthing contract, which guaranteed the first three books with the publisher who had dared to publish *Fishbowl*, was something Noel's London publisher smiled to himself about every morning in the mirror as he brushed his teeth. Thank god he hadn't been stupid enough to turn that one down.

"Are you a keen reader?"

"Yes. Sometimes seems to be the only thing I do."

"Nothing wrong in that. People like me need people like you."

"I bought your book second hand."

"There's no need to get aggressive," Noel poured himself another glass. The number of books he'd sold – especially considering he did only have one published book to his name – meant that he really didn't need to worry about the second hand trade, nor the fact that probably every charity shop in the nation had at least one copy of his book upon its shelves. But he didn't like to think that she had only valued the reading experience at a second hand level.

"Oh, I buy all my books second hand," she added, as if to assure him that she hadn't regretted the pound she'd spent on his work (no royalties for his pocket). "I couldn't afford to buy new all the time."

He wasn't completely pacified by the explanation, but it would have to do. "Well, one must educate oneself. Reading is a great mind opener. I read masses myself these days. Probably all I do. That and drink," he added under his breath at the end.

"And write."

She looked so earnest. 'And write'. Christ, she was naive, he thought to himself. He hadn't written a bloody word since *Fishbowl* had hit the bestseller list. His ideas and his ability seemed to have dried up completely. Which was a terrifying prospect for the man whom the entire world looked to in bated and expectant breath for the follow up.

"I suppose you want to hear about the next book. The book I'm working on."

Noel Farthing's next book. No one knew anything about it. Today was proving to be possibly the best day of her life, Beryl considered, certainly for one who read so much. And she was going to be given exclusive access, an insider's knowledge...

"Well, I shan't tell you," Noel spoke truculently.

Beryl sank back in her chair.

"You've already had access to an entire body of *my* work before we've even met."

"But you're published..." she started, uncertain as to where this mood had come from.

"And what about you? Do you write?"

"Well, yes, but I'm not published." She was conscious of the fact that she was glancing around the patio, checking that there were other people in the vicinity. Witnesses, defenders, players of another part. In case this odd paranoid defensiveness turned nasty. It was very strange, for it was he who had initiated conversation, told her who he was, and ergo opened up his author persona.

"Why not?" It sounded almost like a sneer.

"Well..." she didn't know what to say. Only that she was ready to leave. "I'm not successful like you."

"No, no, no," he leaned forward, impulsively grabbing at her wrist when she jerked the chair back, moving to get up. "I'm making a nasty drunk. We'll have no more of this." He picked up the wine glass and poured the contents onto the ground. "Waiter!" He shouted, stretching his neck like an old tortoise noticing the sun for the first time in months. "Mint tea, here." He didn't bother to check whether the waiter serving the two ancient women had heard him or registered the request – he knew the staff at the hotel was used to him because he spent so much time in Portmeirion. "I need to sober up," he said, returning his attention and the level of his voice back to the young woman at his table. "I need grounding sometimes. Success can make one lose touch with reality now and then. I need to remember what writing's really all about. Tell me, why do you write?"

Beryl was caught on the hop. Settling back into the chair. She hadn't been expecting an interview. Certainly her writing wasn't something she generally spoke to people about. She'd been writing for years, masses of short stories and novels stored away on the hard drive of her laptop. Letters to publishers and agents had come back with the standard generic rejection letter and she had not ventured any further. To talk about her writing with someone who she could be sure had or would actually read it, and risk learning that actually she wasn't that good, was missing the essential spark that couldn't be taught or practiced – simply needed to have been there since the beginning, burning in anticipation at birth – would be to have her bubble burst. Once that was gone, all she would be left with was a mediocre life she wasn't particularly happy with, trudging from one insignificant admin or receptionist job to the next, flat sharing with strangers and never quite having a home or a place of her own. Writing was the only thing that kept her going.

"It's something in me," she finally answered. "I just have these ideas. I just have to get them out."

"How organic," Noel commented. "If you're staying here for three months, you shall have to bring me some of your work to read."

"Oh, I don't know..."

"Three months," Noel sighed, settling back into his seat. "I've been coming here on and off since I was a child. My father – he was a playwright, you know – used to rent one of the flats every summer. Still does, but we tend to plan our arrivals for different times." He coughed, surprised that he was venturing onto a subject he didn't discuss with people. "What do you think of the place?"

"Portmeirion?"

"Yes. The village."

"It's only my first full day here; I've not really explored it that much. It's very pretty, kind of odd though. Like walking through someone else's imagination."

"It's a piece of work, isn't it?"

Beryl couldn't quite tell if Noel meant it as a positive comment or not.

"You'll get to know the place quickly. And the residents, the regulars..."

"I met some of the gardeners this morning."

"Oh, poor you!" Noel burst out, laughing again. He settled into his chair as the waiter appeared at their table with a tray full of tea paraphernalia. "Tell me, you've not met the awful Huw Dodd, have you?" he asked, completely ignoring the presence of the waiter.

Beryl glanced awkwardly at the waiter, who was concentrating most carefully on pouring out the mint tea. A green-amber stream of hot water. The teapot was set down upon the table and the waiter retreated. "I don't remember meeting a Huw this morning."

"Lucky you," Noel said. "He's a miserable bugger. The kind of old bastard who gives Wales a bad name. English hating old git – he can't stand me!" His chair creaked as he leant back, laughing riotously. "Even if you had met him, you won't have realised, because he generally refuses to speak English if he knows you're English. He's not actually left the good green shores of Wales for the last fifteen years. He's the head gardener. Worked here for, goodness, forever. Twenty years at least."

Head gardener. Beryl wondered if Huw Dodd had been one of the men at the table in the staff room this morning.

"Funny thing though, he did give an English man a job. Well, the Portmeirion board were desperate to hire him because he'd worked abroad in Italy a few summers on Italian gardens. This place is dripping in Italian influence, isn't it so? And I suppose they would have overlooked the requirement to speak Welsh, but as luck would have it, the man had learned Welsh for fun. And Huw okayed the contract. Two years ago that was. Huw is a very strange one. Although they're all a bit strange down in the gardening shed. It'll be sniffing those pesticides all day long, I say. Which ones did you meet this morning?"

"Cerys..."

"The eternal optimist."

"...Dafydd..."

"A boy who likes his food."

"...Kev..."

"That scruff is from the kitchens."

She flicked back through the names and faces she had met. And the final man who had entered the building. Tall, thin, elegant. "Adrien."

"Ah!" Noel's eyes lit up. "So you have met the Welsh-speaking Englishman. Odd, isn't it? An Englishman learning Welsh for fun. Although I don't think that's the oddest thing about him."

"What do you mean?"

"Adrien Conway, fluent in English, Welsh and Italian, working as an under gardener in a little North Wales tourist trap. Hardly sounds right for a man with a first class honours degree in architecture, does it? Do you know how many years you have to study to become a fully qualified architect? And he was working for a major international architecture concern. A year into the job, on some obscenely fat wage, and he gives it all up – no reason he's told anyone to my knowledge – and comes back here to take some crumby under gardener job. A shit shoveller."

"He came back here?"

Noel shrugged. "Worked here one summer years ago, just after he'd finished his A-levels. Before he started the architecture dream and the summer jobs in Italy. Bit of a reverse in fortunes, wouldn't you say?"

The light was almost extinguished outside. A last hazy touch before pitch black would wipe out all definition. Beryl was becoming settled in her flat – a kitchen stocked with all the essentials and a late dinner consumed. She was now at a small writing desk in the corner of the living room, shoved out of the way to the side of a slightly-dated brown leather sitting room suite. Her laptop computer was set up at the table, and she'd been looking through her short stories for the last hour, her face illuminated by the dead-white of the computer and the yellow of a table lamp, perched precariously on the edge of the table. She was trying to decide what – if anything – to email to Noel Farthing. The request probably had just been drunken chat, maybe even a guilty conscience after being rude to her. He wouldn't really want to read the ramblings of an amateur – no doubt he was approached by wannabes every day of the week, convinced they were the next Shakespeare, and now that Noel had made it to sucessville, he was duty bound to help all the strugglers up. Either that or he would steal all her ideas and pass them off as his own. Beryl laughed to herself as her imagination ran a little wild. Let's not get carried away.

She finally selected a single short story, a very different style to Noel's own single piece of published work, and emailed it to the address he'd scrawled on a serviette before she could change her mind. How often did anyone get the opportunity to have their work looked at by a name such as Noel Farthing – even if he was already proving to be a slight disappointment. She found it difficult to imagine how the out of shape spoilt rich boy with a drink problem could have created something so exquisitely beautiful as *Fishbowl*.

There, done. She closed the internet explorer screen, her fingers hovering over the keys as if considering to do a little writing. Watching the green bars on the display screen as the computer played the music CD. Not tonight. She felt too unfocused for writing.

Leaning back in the wooden chair, she yawned, stretching her arms out as if reaching for the ceiling. Idly glancing across to the armchair beside her, the red headscarf tossed casually on top of the paper bag of postcards. The postcards – she hadn't given them a thought since arriving in Portmeirion. For stolen goods, she hadn't taken the time to look through and see what little gems might be inside.

Standing up, she took the paper bag and set it on to the glass-topped coffee table in the centre of the three piece suite. Sitting on the edge of the settee, she clasped her hands together in anticipation and peered into the bag. What ought she to do? This was very voyeuristic, and really, she was invading someone's personal space. Perhaps there was someone in Shrewsbury drowning their sorrows in wine, personal mementos lost forever.

There were an awful lot of postcards in this bag, Beryl thought as she removed fistfuls, spreading them out on the coffee table. Picture postcards from across the world, some of the cards a little battered around the edges. Perhaps this was a collection gathered over the years from junk shops and car boot sales. It didn't necessarily mean anything.

She took a card at random. London. Sixteen tiny pictures of some of the well-known sights, all separated by bright yellow dividing lines. The Queen on a horse; Tower Bridge; Nelson's Column; St Paul's; Tower of London. Beryl flicked the postcard over. It had been used, written on and sent.

> It's me. I arrived in London last night. I know it's
> only been a fortnight, and I shouldn't expect too
> much. I think I will go away. I'll stay here until I
> have decided. F

Not exactly the usual 'weather's awful; food's horrid, missing you'. She pulled out a larger card from under a collection. A photo montage again. A clock tower; a modern grey statue; a modern city lay out. Where was it? Beryl turned the card over. The stamp said Chile and the description at the bottom stated Universidad de Concepcion.

> Hola amigo! I know it's been many months. Did
> you think I'd forgotten you? I tried to sever
> contact. But I spent the donkey-trek through the
> mountains thinking about you. I'll stay here for a
> while. I've got a job as an English tutor. I need the
> money desperately. Ffion.

A turquoise sea view with rainforest land. Trinidad and Tobago.

> This place is beautiful. I'm in paradise but it's hell.
> Do you even think about me? I'm on the other
> side of the world and I can find no peace. This will
> be my last card.

Berlin – an evening sky, buildings lit up, street lamps, a concrete statue, curling broken coils.

> I went home with a German man last night. I don't
> speak German. He doesn't speak English. I let him
> have me three times. I think I'm free of this. Ffion.

A picture of the side of an aeroplane.

> I'm on the plane to Helsinki. They had these cards
> in the pocket in front. I am wanting to get away
> from the familiar. I thought somewhere colder. I
> don't really know anything about Finland. Ffion.

A stately building in an historic city, by the river. It didn't look familiar. Everything printed on the back was in the Cyrillic alphabet. She guessed the country was Russia.

> Do you remember that evening after the party
> when we bumped into each other at the Atlas
> statue? I keep thinking about it. Wishing myself
> back – I had such hopes then. Happy, happy times.
> My memories keep me warm as the nights draw
> in. Ffion.

This wasn't a random find in a junkshop, the total collection of some stranger's years' worth of trawling through scrappy shoeboxes of used postcards, five pence each. These were all part of one person's story. The handwriting was the same, cards signed either by Ffion, F or no signature. Beryl wasn't sure if Ffion was a male or female name, but there was a definite femininity to the writing style. This was a story. She flicked back through the postcards she had already read. The dates that these cards had been sent on ranged over a period of several years, and she hadn't been reading them in order. What a curious treasure trove. One she shouldn't have in her possession. The cards had all been sent to a place called Bryn Bwbach – she'd never heard of it, but the name looked Welsh. Perhaps the bag had been left by someone who'd been on the same route as she had, only in the opposite direction, Wales to Shrewsbury.

She picked up a card of a city in the woods, marked out as Canberra, Australia.

> Oh god, I don't know what to do. I arrived late and I couldn't find anywhere to stay so I thought I'd just walk along the river. This man attacked me. I never knew it could hurt that much. I'm now staying in a dump too scared to go out. Oh god, Huw, will you come and get me? I don't have enough money to get home. This travelling isn't solving anything. Please! Ffion.

Beryl dropped the postcard as if it had bitten her. A woman had been raped, and sent a postcard back to Wales to a man called Huw – she hadn't gone to the police, or the hospital in Australia; she hadn't even called someone. She'd written to a man, presumably the same person all these postcards were addressed to. Years' worth of travelling documented and sent back to someone. There was a problem that the travelling was supposed to rectify, but the writer was learning that running away wasn't solving anything. And in the worst moments, her immediate thoughts were of this man. Thoughts bagged up and abandoned in a railway station. This postcard was six years old. Had Huw gone to Australia to save Ffion? She didn't suppose she'd ever know.

Wandering back to the computer, which was in hibernation mode, Beryl pushed back the screen, waking the machine up. Just idle curiosity, she said to herself. She googled Bryn Bwbach. Where was it?

She came to a map, roads with nothing marked. If she went on street view it was just a few houses spread out in the countryside. Single track roads hemmed in with stone walls and hedges. But where? Returning to the map, she zoomed out. The coastline swiftly appeared, a river inlet and there was Portmeirion.

Portmeirion. Bryn Bwbach must be only a fifteen minute drive away from where she was now. Beryl hurried back to the postcards. There was more that was unnervingly familiar. What was it? She flicked back through the postcards. All from the same woman, to the same man. Won't you go and save her? Huw, will you save me? Huw Dodd from Bryn Bwbach in Gwynedd. Did you go to Australia and rescue Ffion?

Beryl slumped back into the settee. "No," she said to herself. He didn't rescue Ffion. Huw Dodd hadn't done anything. She remembered where she recognised the name now. For Huw Dodd was the head gardener at Portmeirion, and as Noel Farthing had informed her earlier in the day, Huw Dodd hadn't left Wales for the last fifteen years.

The guidebook was, to put it politely, a little dry. Certainly a well-designed, glossy booklet full of brightly coloured photographs showing off the infinite artistic angles the village could be viewed from. That was the main selling feature. Photographs taken on a sunny day that were of a higher standard than most tourists could manage. Architectural history and ponderings hadn't really been her topic of interest, and she guessed a lot of people who bought the book would gloss over the text. At least there was only half of the writing to read, should she feel that she ought to study the booklet cover to cover, for there was also a great deal in Welsh.

Early evening, Beryl was exploring beyond the main body of the village. She'd walked past the hotel, down along by the coast, passing statues, miniature lighthouses, and into the forest, coming to the head of the peninsula. This area was part of the Portmeirion estate, but it was beyond the formal control of the village board, a natural forest tamed by some human influence. Great rhododendron shrubs, the blooms now well past their best, filled up the space between trees like great heavy organic clouds of greenery. The track led down to a large pond, weeping willows drizzling into the water. The light was a little husky. Beryl meandered along the track, the guidebook held down by her side, occasionally lifted to waft away insects.

There was a red Japanese wooden bridge across a narrow section of the pond. Footsteps thudding over the wooden plank like an out of tune xylophone. Continuing up the side of the pond. She could hear voices in the wood. Not particularly loud, a little tense. Words not wasted for the sake of it. Close enough for her to be able to make out the words and realise it was Welsh being spoken.

She stepped on a dry twig, which snapped; the sound embarrassingly loud. The talking stopped. Beryl spotted the two gardeners across the far side of the pond, part way up the wooded bank. Spades were dug into the earth like markers, the digging complete for the time being. An unhealthy looking large bush was at an on odd angle, probably half way out of the ground and on its way to the compost heap. Further down, on the track near the water, there was a little trailer truck with a large rhododendron plant in a black tub.

Two men at work, one stood: Adrien Conway, whom she had briefly met the other morning; and another crouched over the roots of the dying bush. An older man, forties or fifties – Beryl wasn't sure – that she remembered having been at the table in the staff room.

Both men stopped what they were doing and looked over at her. The elder, in his misshapen woollen jumper stood up and started jabbering in Welsh, gesticulating. She didn't understand, but judging from the raised volume and the arm waving, he was saying something to her. Beryl stopped and stared across at the two gardeners. What was their problem? This wood was open to the public, and there certainly hadn't been any signs to say it was closed for maintenance.

"Huw," Adrien spoke, looking a little irritated, with Huw, with Beryl, and the fact that he had to be there out in the woods at all. "She doesn't speak Welsh."

Beryl felt a little affronted. Adrien made it sound as though it was doubtful about her speaking English as well; the way he over pronounced every word in the sentence as if it was for her dumb benefit.

"Oh of course," Huw switched easily between languages, his Welsh accent particularly strong on the English words. The tone was irritation, anger, which didn't match the sing-song rhythm of his dialect. "Bugger off, will you," he called crossly to Beryl. "Don't you know the village shuts at seven?"

"But I'm staying here."

"I don't care," Huw retorted. "What do you think we are? Here for your entertainment?"

"But I didn't..."

"Are you going to get going then?"

A burning red flush rushed up her face. Beryl turned and hurried onwards along the path away from the pond. She heard Adrien mutter something in Welsh to Huw. She hadn't done anything wrong, hadn't done anything, yet the man was aggressive and offensive as if she'd kicked dirt in his face, spat on him and demanded he polish her shoes. She ought to have told him to fuck off. Either that or stubbornly sat down on one of the benches by the pond, and watch them plant that bloody bush. If he was so vain to think that people were actually interested enough in what he was doing to want to watch, she should have stayed for the performance. Instead off she ran like an awkward child, which only made her feel even more embarrassed.

The forest track came out on a dead-end tarmac road behind what was referred to as the town hall. She followed the track up to a wider space in front of the now-closed cafe. The only thought she had was to keep moving, not wanting to bump into the gardeners again. She didn't even know why they were still working – the working day started so early for them; surely they would have gone home by now. Beryl turned to her right and headed down the road, past the village hall, the bookshop, the strange petrol pump with modelled head on a pole, and towards the hotel, passing the round, intensely blue swimming pool to her left. Through the parking zone and turning area that marked the end of the road, she moved around to the front of the hotel, feeling the sea breeze coming down the estuary. Back to the patio wall where she had first been accosted by Noel Farthing.

Down below on the next level, the white ship was built into the sea wall. The tide was in and the ship clung hesitantly to the wall, as if considering pulling up anchor and leaving the port for the wider world. The words *Amis Reunis* were painted on the side of the black hull. The light was starting to fade, and a few lamps had been atmospherically hung around the ship, including a couple in the two cabins on deck. A figure sat on a stool in the doorway of the little cabin in front of the mast, hunched over a guitar but not playing. Another was slouched on the ship wall closest to the hotel, facing out to sea. The bright orange prick of burning embers on the end of a cigarette glowed against the evening.

Beryl let out a sigh. The almost shapeless human figure sat on the wall took the cigarette away from lips, and, blowing out a thin plume of smoke, looked up the steps to the hotel patio. "*Noswaith dda*," the figure said, the voice betraying it was female. The figure in the cabin snorted and looked up. Beryl realised it was Noel Farthing.

Welsh again. "I don't speak..." Beryl started.

"Neither do I," Noel's voice boomed out. "Speak your master's language, girl."

The cigarette end was flicked to the ground and stubbed out underfoot. "*Cachau bant*," the woman laughed, not unkindly, but confident in the knowledge that present company didn't understand. Beryl realised the woman with the cigarette was Cerys, the gardener. "Is that you up there, Beryl?" Cerys asked, squinting against the darkening sky. "Come on down." She bent forward, picking up a pint glass that was set on the concrete floor. "We're having a bit of a jamming session here," she added, laughing into her drink.

Beryl walked down the steps from the patio. "It seems very quiet for a jamming session."

"Noel thinks he's found a new outlet for his artistic frustration," Cerys explained as Beryl sat down on the exterior wall near her.

"I'll have you know I had lessons to play this when I was a boy."

"He went into Porthmadog today," Cerys continued, ignoring Noel. "Did the charity shops and came home with a second hand guitar. It's not even in tune, but he can't hear it."

"It sounds just dandy to me," Noel strummed through the six strings. The two women winced at the sound.

"Have you met Noel, by the way?" Cerys asked.

"Oh yes," Noel answered on Beryl's behalf. "We have already met. Not only that, but we are kindred writers..."

Beryl winced. She didn't usually like to tell people that she wrote in her free time. It was a well-kept secret, and she'd only admitted it the other day because it had been Noel Farthing who had asked. It was the sort of opportunity that most people never got, and it felt like smacking experience in the face to not go with the flow. But she didn't like the way he freely scattered her secrets like pennies, as if they had been his to begin with.

"Interesting stuff, by the way," he added as an aside. "We must reconvene sometime on the subject."

"You write?" Cerys looked pleased by the revelation. She liked interesting people. "It's good to have a method of expression. I do a little sculpting and a lot of gardening."

"And I play the guitar," Noel added.

"Play isn't quite the word."

"All right smart arse, you play us a tune." Rather off handed, Noel gripped the guitar by the neck and pointed it at Cerys. "The Welsh are supposed to be musical. Male voice choirs and all that."

"And I'm not a man and a guitar isn't singing. How about you?"

Beryl shrugged. "A few chords, but nothing special."

"That makes you the most qualified on board." Cerys took the instrument from Noel and passed it to Beryl.

"As long as she's not going to play bridge over bloody water," Noel grumbled. Illuminated by Moroccan tin lamps, his messy hair highlighted by the warm light, he looked over at Beryl, who had somewhat shyly crossed her legs and draped herself around the guitar.

"You don't like Simon and Garfunkel?"

"All the wannabes sing that song."

"A guitar isn't singing." She didn't know many songs, and most of those she knew were people such as Simon and Garfunkel, Gordon Lightfoot and other acoustic types her mother enjoyed listening to. She'd had a slightly hippie upbringing. "And this really needs tuning," she added, thumbing at the G string. Listening to every string one by one, she could tell everything vibrated at the wrong level, but knowing where to start was a talent she didn't have.

"Ahoy sailor!" Noel suddenly blared.

Footsteps along the dusky sea front headed towards the little gathering. Beryl squinted through the weakening light, watching the tall figure approach. A breeze brushed over the loose shirt, marking out a slender figure. Shaggy hair. Ah, Adrien Conway. She looked back at the guitar. She'd only recently seen him in the woods with Huw Dodd, when the two gardeners had been unpleasant. She hoped he wasn't going to bring the incident up, and embarrass her in front of Cerys and Noel. She couldn't imagine Cerys or Noel standing for such behaviour, and didn't want to see their pitying or mocking responses to the incident.

"Adrien," Cerys greeted the gardener as he stepped into the ship's entrance, a narrow break in the wall, with a woman on either side. "Has Huw finally let you finish for the day?"

"Finally." Adrien nodded, stuffing his hands into his pockets and leaning back into himself, rolling on his heels. He looked out onto the darkening estuary. "He's been in a particularly shitty mood today."

"When is he not?" Noel drolly commented. He picked up his red wine from the cabin window sill and took a drink. "So the cultured one is with us," he continued. "Will you join us proles? Beryl was just going to give us a tune."

"Beryl's not," she decided, slapping her hand against the strings. "This is very badly out of tune and I am too sleepy to even try to fix it."

"Is it yours?" Adrien asked, reaching for it as she set it up vertical on her knee as if to play it like a double bass.

"No, it's mine," Noel's voice came from the cabin.

Adrien's fingers hesitated around the guitar's neck for a moment, as if unsure whether to snatch it away or push it back in Beryl's face. "You taking up music, Noel?"

"I might do," Noel said, something in his voice suggesting the idea was already wearing thin. "A man has to try these things now and then. Don't tell us you're an accomplished guitarist too? How many strings do you have on your bow?"

"I dabble." Adrien settled on taking the guitar from Beryl. He sat down in the doorway to the larger cabin on the ship's deck. Hunching over the guitar like a vampire, listening carefully to the sound of single strings.

"Something of an expert dabbler," Noel muttered. "We should call you a duck. Dabbling in every pond."

Beryl looked over at Noel, who was steadily watching Adrien. Was it just her imagination, or was there a touch of hostility in the air? She looked to Cerys for some kind of confirmation, but Cerys' mind seemed to be elsewhere as she smiled to herself and sipped her cider.

Conversation fizzled out; no one wanted to talk. Beryl felt uncomfortable and something of an intruder. She had not yet been here a week, whereas these people had known one another on and off for years. If there was any disagreement, it had nothing to do with her, and she did not want to get involved. She stretched out her feet, looking down at her shoes, then to the village guide book she was still carrying. Opened the front cover and looked through the publishing information at the front. Apparently someone called Ffion Owen had written the Welsh text. She looked up sharply. Ffion had been the name on the postcards.

"Is Ffion a man or a woman's name?"

Immediately the atmosphere thickened, and Beryl wished she hadn't asked. It was painful, the others looking as though they wanted to pretend there was no connection to the name, nothing to be upset over. The sound of Cerys setting her pint glass on the concrete floor was painfully loud. "It's a woman's name," she answered neutrally.

Noel was peering at Beryl now; Adrien and the guitar forgotten. "Why on earth would you ask something like that?"

The village held its breath. Beryl wished she'd walked straight home after bumping into Adrien and Huw in the woods. She ought to have taken it as an omen that this evening was not going to be a good one. "It's just a name listed in the credits of this book," she said feebly.

"Ah, that must be Ffion Owen you're asking about?" Noel said.

A loud strum through reasonably in-tune strings broke off Noel's opportunity to continue that line of discussion. Adrien started to play, teetering on the boundary between idly jamming and actually playing a specific tune. The melody sounded familiar, although Beryl couldn't quite think of the song or the artist. But Adrien was obviously more than a dabbler in music, judging by the way his fingers plucked swiftly through the notes, without pause or uncertainty. Music, languages and architecture – it screamed over-achiever. Certainly Noel would win in the success stakes, he did have one of the best selling pieces of literature from the last hundred years under his belt, but Noel did strike her as a bit of a one trick pony, and she could understand why he might find people like Adrien irritating. Perhaps that was why he had taken to her so immediately and easily. There wasn't anything to be jealous of.

Beryl snapped her guidebook shut and stood up, suddenly decided and tired of being polite for other people's sake. "I'm going to head back now," she told the others. "I'm tired."

Adrien stopped playing anything specific, and switched to indiscriminate chords. "It must be tiring doing nothing all day."

The light was poor, and she couldn't really see his expression, as he was coiled over the guitar. She couldn't tell if his comment was meant unkindly or just a friendly joke. But the others neither backed him up nor told him to mind his manners, and Beryl felt she'd overstayed her welcome on board this evening.

"Be seeing you."

Warm golden sun. A reassuring caress over skin formed of sunlight. The sound of a skylark retreating up into the endless blue skies. White clouds skeltering across the heavens. The weightless summer breeze whipping over the hills, rustling through the long, uncut meadow grass. Dislodging a bumble bee from a cornflower.

Beryl smiled, stretching like a cat in the warmth. She opened her eyes, gazed at the glowing blue sky. Sitting up, she regarded her surroundings. Ahead there was plain of hummock-shaped hills, domes of child-like design, grass laden and bathed in golden light. Far in the distance the sea glittered; a breathing blue body of tiny diamond specks. She placed her hands in the grass to push herself up onto her feet. Brushed down her skirts, noticing her curious attire for the first time. A full length dress, skirts heavy with drapes and layers; all cast in red polka dots, a ribbon fixed around a high waist, a corseted bodice to make her waist as small as possible, a bustle tied low around her hips to make the lower half suitably vague. A bustle? Beryl twisted around, aware of the dead weight attached to her body, like an extreme sweater tied around the hips to hide a large posterior, but only increasing the lack of proportion. How odd, and how ungainly did it make her figure? She tried to examine it, craning over her own shoulder, and ended up chasing her own tail up on the hill.

Spinning to a halt, she looked back towards the coast, a little town, a mere village, by the sea, rooftops barely visible. Thank god no one was here to see her acting like a fool. Feeling her straw bonnet glide forward towards her forehead, threatening to topple off, she pushed the hat back a little. Her hair was full of curls and pinned up, a straw hat of decorative size that served no other use balanced on top of her intricate hairstyle. The hat was tied in place with a ribbon under her chin.

Her luggage was at her feet. She picked up her belongings – the small quaint trug full of handpicked wildflowers (rather impractical for a travelling woman) and a rather more substantial carpet bag. As she was straightening, carpet bag in one hand, trug weightlessly hung over the crook of the other elbow, two things occurred to her. Right now, she thought to herself, I am living in my own mind. That and she looked like a cliché off a biscuit tin of shortbread.

She could not recall having been in such a vivid dream before. Stepping decisively forward, she marched in the direction of the little village. Hopeful, and quite determined to explore as much as possible.

Nearing the village, it was clear that the coastline functioned as a natural sea defence of high ravaged cliffs. There was only one building truly at the top, set a good distance away from the village. A manor house, darkened on the edge, keen to be overlooked. The village itself was situated in what looked like half a crater bitten out of the cliffs, a steep slope rolling down towards the little port and sea level. Even the houses at the far reaches of the village didn't want to be on cliff level, instead cut into the ground a metre or so downwards. Quaint, rickety little fishing cottages built before the invention of spirit levels lined the narrow winding street down into the cliff and towards the shore. Beryl felt elated, near-skipping down the cobbled cart track, no particular destination or goal, merely revelling in exploration.

She passed a couple of fishermen sat on crates fixing nets. Outside a cottage, wooden lobster pots and blue twine for netting hung on the wall. They looked up as the stranger walked by. How odd, they bore a strong resemblance to Kev and Dafydd. She didn't think much of it until she reached what must have been the centre of the village; a cobbled square with a stone market cross and an ornate water pump with a rock-carved trough in the centre. A rotund man in rather more formal attire than a fisherman was puffing his way up through the village, a ruddiness to his cheeks that increased with the incline. Sunlight glanced off the silver buckles on his shoes, skimmed off the wide rim of his hat. He tilted the aforementioned headwear to Beryl, grinning at her and unashamedly checking the size of her bustle as he passed. Beryl paused and looked back, watching his retreating figure. Hadn't that been Noel Farthing?

Perhaps it was due to lack of imagination that she had to borrow people she already knew for this fantasy. The final piece of evidence turned up when she rounded the corner, coming upon a three-storey inn, The Seagull Inn to be precise, with diamond leaded windows and the lady inn keeper outside shaking off a mat. Cerys, but a distinctly more feminine version, with an inflated bosom and a corseted medieval wench dress. She draped the mat over one arm as Beryl approached.

"Good morrow, stranger," she called to her. "Are you looking for somewhere to stay? You've come to the right place. The Seagull Inn is a highly reputable place and a boarding house. Very fine for all travellers. I'm the innkeeper. Arabella."

Beryl squinted at her. "Cerys?"

"Cerys? Very nice to make your acquaintance. I have just the room for you..."

"No, I..." she started, but Arabella (Cerys) had already turned her back and was leading the way into the wooden interiors of the inn, a hotchpotch of tiny rooms, unbelievably narrow staircases, corridors and angulated ceilings that defied common sense.

"...and all my rooms are watertighted so you needn't worry on that account..." Arabella (Cerys) was saying as she hitched up her skirts out of feet's way to ascend the staircase. She led Beryl up to the top floor and down the corridor to a room at the side of the inn. How quaint, Beryl thought, all the doors had round handles with spokes, like the steering wheel on old galleons.

"There we are, Miss Cerys."

"Please, it's Beryl."

"Of course," Arabella (Cerys) winked. "Miss Beryl Cerys."

It was a pleasant room, even if Beryl was only able to stand up straight in the very middle. There was a neat bed with thick patchwork blanket that looked incredibly inviting. A small washstand and dressing table were at one side. Then a square window of thick glass that offered a view onto the little streets and the sea in the distance. Beryl set her trug of flowers on the windowsill.

"Is it not a fine room?"

Beryl turned from the window. "Very fine. I'll take it."

"Excellent."

She placed her carpet bag at the foot of the bed. "I think I might walk around the village a little now."

"As you wish, but mind you watch the turn," Arabella (Cerys) winked at her, oblivious to the fact that Beryl clearly had no idea what she was talking about. "And if you don't care to retreat to your room, for it is early today, my parlour is fully up to date with plenty of seating for all my patrons."

What a strange woman, Beryl thought as she left the inn. Did she think she might be considering retiring for the night soon? It was only the afternoon.

Following the natural incline downwards, she passed cottages blanketed in honeysuckle, others with glass buoys for pots and nets hung decoratively at the door frame. Rounding a corner, there was a beautiful smell of fresh pine wood. A man sat on a half-log bench, witling something from a piece of wood. Shavings scattered on the ground around his feet. He looked up as she came down the alley; it was Adrien – he had to be somewhere she supposed. He smiled gently at her, then returned to his work.

Beryl reached the seafront; a little harbour with a neat wooden fence running along the front. Someone had spent a lot of time decorating the fencing with seaweed, the glistening green strands twined around and around. It ought to have smelt salty and a little rank, but she didn't notice any unpleasant aromas. Neither was it slimy, instead rather velvety to the touch. She looked out to the water. There were stone steps down to the shore, but the tide was in and the riches of the natural coastline were hidden for the time being. She smiled to no one and felt the sun on her face. It was so peaceful, so pretty here.

She followed the harbour front, then took a small track up to a little stone church. Through the graveyard and to the main door, but it was locked. She would have to explore it in another dream, another day.

Retracing her steps, she headed back for the harbour. The cobble stones seemed more glistening and lustrous than she recalled. Rounding the corner to the lowest past of the harbour, she slowed to a halt, staring in horror at the water. The section of the harbour where the stone steps had descended to the beach was now submerged. The waves lapped up and over, with every undulation the water level seemed to rise a centimetre or so. The tide's still coming in, she thought. The seaweed on the lower rungs of the fence, now underwater, flowed out like hair. Barnacles breathed in the salt water. Beryl looked over her shoulder back to the ally to the church. There had been a tall spire, but the door had been locked. Even if she ran back, she wouldn't get in for shelter.

Panicking, she looked back to the water, which was already lapping at her boots. The water glittered aquamarine. I'll just have to wade through it, she thought miserably, stepping into the surprisingly warm water. It immediately drenched her already heavy and multinous skirts, making them lead weights dragging down from her hips. She felt the pull of the tide swell up around her legs, pushing her first towards the front row of houses, then back towards the harbour fence with breathing regularity. At its deepest it reached her hips, swirling water that almost looked painted.

It was like walking in concrete boots, slow and not nearly quick enough against the rate of the tide. As she rounded the end of the harbour, she could see the water steadily creeping up the narrow road into the main body of the village. Her clothing was so heavy; she could have easily just slipped backwards as if falling into a bed of feathers. She pushed herself onwards, gasping, feeling the water pour from her clothes as she began to gain a little altitude, emerging from the sea. There was a rumbling behind and a particularly large wave rushed up, taking the water level back to her ankles just as she'd broken free.

"Oh no!" Beryl staggered forward, gripping her skirts as if pulling free of thorns. She would have run but she was too weighted down.

She rounded the corner, the tide at her heels. Adrien had just tied the wooden bench to the side of his cottage and was about to retreat inside. He looked shocked to see Beryl stumbling up the road. Without a word he darted out, grabbing her arm and pulling her into the cottage. Slamming the door shut, turning the key. Beryl looked aghast at the front door as water started to trickle under the threshold.

"We'll be drowned!"

Still silent, he virtually threw her in through an open doorway to the right. There was a loud slam as he pulled the door to, spinning the door handle, a wheel such as those she had seen in the inn. A click, then he stopped, breathing heavily. "That was close," he finally said.

Beryl was shivering. "What's happening?"

"We'll have to wait it out for the next few hours." He turned to look at her. Her wet dress hung heavy. "You might want to get out of those wet clothes."

She wasn't really listening. Looking around the room. A neat room, relaxing blue coloured wallpaper. Fine landscape paintings hung. A small, but respectable marble fireplace. Lamp fittings on the wall for oil burners – electricity didn't exist here. A couple of armchairs by the fire, a small bookcase, a wardrobe, and a large double bed. He'd dragged her in here without a word, locked the door, said they would be there for hours and suggested she get undressed. Oh Christ.

Adrien must have guessed from the look on her face what she was thinking. He was horrified to realise that someone would consider him capable of such underhand lack of respect towards a woman. "I don't mean you any harm," he assured her. "Only that your dress is saturated. I think you must have been caught out by the tide. I don't wish you to become ill. You could at least take the outer dress off – please use the bedspread for coverings. I could start a fire to dry your dress. I will turn my back." He abruptly stepped up to the fireplace, his back resolutely to her.

It made perfect sense, but Beryl was still giddy from her tangle with the water, still unsure as to what was happening. She took off her little straw hat and threw it at the bed. Looking desperately down at her waist, turning one way then the other, she realised she had no idea how to get out of this dress. It was so close fitting it certainly wasn't going to pull up over her head. Pathetically she dropped onto a stool by the window, ready to cry. What was she supposed to do? Ask him to undress her. "I..."

"You?" He turned, cautiously at first as if she might already be in a state of undress. "Oh, I see," he said, realising the issue. "Well, I..." he looked nervously around the room. "Yes!" he picked up a pail from the corner and set it by the fire. "Come sit here. I'll light a fire. We can wring the worst of the water out."

She approached the fire, carefully settled herself in one of the armchairs. Looked over to the window near the bed. Through the glass all she could see was blue, with swirls of vivid golden threads, like sunlight, twisting and moving, almost pushing up against the glass. She looked back to Adrien, who was crouched at the fireplace, stacking a few cut logs into the grate. "We're submerged, aren't we?"

The first smoulders of a fire starting. "The roof will soon be under if not already."

"And this room..."

"It's watertight."

Just as all the rooms in the Seagull Inn. That was what Arabella (Cerys) had been referring to. "This water goes all the way through the village?"

Adrien stepped back from the little fire. "Why yes." He looked curiously at her. "You didn't know?"

She shook her head and stared miserably at her skirts as she started to wring sea water out of the fabric.

"You can only just have arrived," he commented. "For even visitors learn quickly. It's difficult to miss when it happens every day."

"Every day?" Beryl was horrified.

"Yes. But sometimes at night."

This wasn't quite the paradise she'd imagined when she'd viewed it from the tops of the hills. "I must thank you for your generosity," she said, looking down into the pail. "For I don't know what I would have done otherwise."

"If you'd had the strength, you would have run out of the village," he said. "The water does stop at the cliffs. It never has the strength to breach those. But please do not worry; I am honoured by your visit."

If this was the Adrien of Portmeirion, such a comment would have been said with sarcasm; but this version, this much nicer version of the man, was quite genuine. She smiled.

"Forgive me for being so bold," he started. "But we've not been introduced."

She laughed. "No, I don't believe we have. I'm Beryl," she started. "Miss Beryl Cerys." She might as well keep some semblance of continuity in all of this madness, she supposed, repeating her ridiculous new name that the innkeeper had christened her with.

"Rufus," he introduced himself.

"Rufus," Beryl repeated, thinking this was going to get confusing. "And it will be a few hours before the tide recedes?"

"Oh yes."

She looked into the flames. The fire was crackling. "Will the water not come down the chimney?"

Rufus (Adrien) smiled patiently at her; she really knew nothing about coastal life. "I have an adaptor fitted. We're quite safe." He stumbled upwards to a casket on top of the bookcase. "I might offer some refreshment. I have some crumpets here we could toast by the fire."

"That would be very kind." Beryl looked back to the window, jolting into the support of her armchair when she saw a woman's face staring in at them. Hair swirling with the movement of the tide. She looked calm, actually smiling and not in a rush to surface. Hardly drowning. She looked away from the porthole into the little room, as if hearing something deeper in the water. Then with a flick of silver scales, she was gone.

Mermaids, Beryl thought. I've just seen a mermaid.

PART TWO

The Train Journey

When they got on the train in Porthmadog, north Wales, the sky overhead was cloudy and threatening drizzle. Their escape pod on tracks pulled in through the damp air; it looked like a local train; only two carriages, but with the final destination of Birmingham in the front window. This train intended to cover some miles.

David glanced at his watch, thinking of the long hours before they would reach Birmingham. There they would change to a national train to get home. For now they were on the long distance local train that intended to stop at every tiny, god-forsaken platform in Wales.

Heaving his long hiking rucksack into the luggage shelves by the door, he followed his girlfriend up the near empty train carriage to a table seat. His satchel was slung diagonally round his body – all the essentials crammed inside: money, credit cards, i-pod, mobile phone, books, roll up ciggie papers and tobacco bag, gum, mints, chocolate bars, condoms, maps and the precious baby of the group: his digital camera.

He slumped into the window seat on the opposite side of the table to his girlfriend, Eliza. She gazed grimly back out to the platform. The eyebrow piercing she'd had for the last six months seemed to weight down her face as she regarded the sky.

"Looks like it's going to piss it down," she muttered.

"Maybe not. It seems to get cloudy here a lot without raining."

"True," she sighed. "Well, at least it waited until we are going home."

David stretched his legs out diagonally to the opposing aisle seat. Scratched his short beard and looked out of the window. The journey here had been just as long, but the sun had been blazing and they had been excited for the holiday. The train line came through the Welsh hills before running up the coast, and the views had been particularly good. They had ooed and aahed at the rocks, mountains, greenery and dramatic imposing views, but even fantastic scenery can get boring after a while. He had taken a lot of photographs, but when you get to shot one hundred of a craggy hillside, you can start having trouble distinguishing it from craggy hillside shot number seventy two.

Light drizzle smacked against the carriage window. Sea fret pulled in towards the shore. The carriages jolted at the sound of the engine revving up vibrating down the length of the train. They started to pull away from Porthmadog.

"I think I'm going to sleep for a bit."

"Right then," Eliza said, monotone. She already had that flea bitten journal out, pen poised to begin scribbling. That thing again. David saw it as a throw back to her teenage days. She was twenty-two; she ought to get over all that self-obsessing analysis. Still, she probably wouldn't have time for the thing when they got back and she started her new job.

He nodded off quickly, leaving it to Eliza to deal with the ticket inspector. He woke up for a short period as the train stopped in Barmouth. The clouds had really pulled in, casting the world in grey-scale. It didn't appear to be raining, but it looked distinctly damp outside. Cold. Very uninviting.

Eliza was reading — a glossy paperback of inoffensive and uninspired writing voted as great stuff by some chocolaty plump women's book club. He didn't know why she wasted her time with books like that, but she said she enjoyed them. David closed his eyes. They were still several hours away from Birmingham.

The next time he woke up the train was at a complete standstill. He blinked groggily. There was no movement. The absence of the steady hum through the carriage body suggested the engines had been switched off. He remembered from the original journey that they had had to stop so that the train could split in two. Perhaps they were waiting for the other half to arrive.

It was very misty outside, visibility low. He couldn't see very far at all. The mist rolled and throbbed up against the window as if it was alive. Bloody depressing. What a way to end the holiday.

He stretched his arms and yawned widely. "Have we been stopped long?"

Eliza ignored the question and just stared down her nose at him. She was sat a funny angle, her head leant back and tilted so it rested against the window. Her eyelids lowered in a condescending look. She viewed him but said nothing.

"What's your problem? You in a sulk again?"

No reply.

There was definitely something out of place. The way her long hair seemed to be glued to her chest. The way her top wasn't as brightly coloured as he remembered. He leaned forward, looking through the scattered clutter of necklaces around her neck. "Oh shit," he hissed, reaching out but stopping fingers mere centimetres from her neck. He had thought it was a choker. It was a wound, a gaping slice going right into her throat. The sticky wetness caking her was blood. "Shit!" he said loudly, jumping away as if she was going to bite. His mind was a blank. Disorientated. What was he supposed to do in a situation like this? I've just woken up on a train, my girlfriend is dead and her throat is gaping.

He stood up abruptly. "Hello? Help?"

The carriage was empty.

David hurried down the aisle to the end of the carriage. It was the end of the train. The toilet door was open, the cubicle empty. He turned around, feeling desperate. The ticket collector had to be here. The driver. Someone. He ran back up the carriage, trying not to look at Eliza, and pushed through into the front carriage. There was no one here. Not even a discarded newspaper. Absolutely nothing. He went to the head of the train and forced his way into the driver's compartment.

Empty.

What the fuck? He turned back to the carriage, feeling his bowels weaken. Come on; don't lose your nerve now. He clenched. There had to be an explanation.

He shivered, feeling the chill creep up around him. He hadn't noticed before, but all the doors were open. That must be it; everyone had got off the train. What else were you going to do when someone had been murdered? But why had they left him? Had they tried to wake him up? Maybe they had thought he was dead as well.

David poked his head out of the carriage door. This place gave him the creeps. There was not a sound. A short platform, edged in thick white blocks, gravelled in the centre. At the back ran a wire fence with a small wooden gate breaking the thin lines. A country track in grass ran off beyond. Gorse bushes hung over the top of the fencing. Beyond that he couldn't see very much; the mist was so thick.

"Hello?"

He sounded stupid. Gingerly, he got down from the train, his boots crunching on the gravel. He walked past the wooden station sign – the name unpronounceable Welsh to him – and went to the closest end of the platform. It ended abruptly in a vertical drop. The train lines went off into the mist.

He turned around. "Is anyone there?" he yelled. He sounded like a twat. He walked to the other end of the platform, which also ended in a vertical drop.

There was a hiss as the carriage doors shut, thumping as they met in the middle. The engines groaned. David looked uncertainly over his shoulder. The engines revved up and the two carriages gave a jolt. There wasn't supposed to be anyone on that train.

"Hey, hey, hey!" he shouted as the carriages started to pull away from the platform. He ran at the side, hammering his fists at the windows, pushing at the open buttons on the doors which refused to give way. Eliza passed him, still leaning against the window, unmoving. David ran after the train but could not board it. He staggered to a halt at the end of the platform and watched the train disappear into the thick mist.

Completely alone. He looked around, a knot in his throat. He felt near to tears, abandoned. Gulped and wiped at the corner of his eyes. Grow up. Be a man. He didn't know what to do at all. What were you supposed to do in god-knew-where when a train carrying the corpse of your girlfriend had driven off, as if by magic, into the thick fog?

Opening his satchel, he took out his mobile phone. He wasn't surprised to see there wasn't any reception. Besides, the battery had almost run down to zero. He'd forgotten to recharge it last night. Shit.

He ran to the station sign. It meant nothing to him. He took out his maps, tracing the route of the train, looking for this station. It wasn't there. He couldn't even look for some obvious landmark, for everything was hidden by the mist.

Shit shit shit. He tried to re fold the map, but his hands were shaking, and once these giant sheets of paper were unfolded, they were virtually impossible to reassemble even in calmer moments. He screamed at nothing and crumpled the map up into a sulky mess, stuffing it into his satchel.

Still there was nothing.

Perhaps there was a village close by. There must be something, why else have a station? He walked to the gate at the back of the platform, clutched the top, and looked uncertainly back. All alone now. Eliza was dead. Gone. It hit him for the first time. She had annoyed the hell out of him at times, but he had loved her. In his own way.

Dead.

Murdered.

He bit his lip. Now wasn't the time to break down.

He pushed open the gate and started down the dirt track between the gorse bushes. Winding to suit nature. The mist swirled. The platform behind soon disappeared. He felt as though he were in a maze, the tall, inpenetrative walls of the gorse forcing him in only one direction. He walked for five minutes, then stopped. This was ridiculous. For all he knew, this could be a hiking track up into the mountains. This could take him hours away from any civilisation.

He looked back and a wall of fog greeted him. He didn't like this at all. He wanted to be back at the station.

He had half expected the platform not to be there when he returned. The only marker, the only point of stability in this mess. He walked up and down the length of the platform, looking for a timetable, for thrown away tickets, cigarette butts, any sign of life. There was nothing but the station sign.

He sat down on the platform, feeling giddy. His mind was rushing, his breathing getting faster. Was this a panic attack? He didn't feel that he could cope.

Calm down.

He needed something to calm down.

Sitting on the edge of the platform, legs hanging over the white edging stones, he took his digital camera out of the satchel. Better memories of a holiday just passed. He flicked it onto view mode and turned the camera on. The most recently taken photograph showed up on the miniature screen.

Eliza stared at the camera. The blood congealing down her chest. Her skin drained of blood, now white. Dead glassy eyes. He hadn't taken this photograph. David gagged.

He flicked back to the photo before. Eliza again. Still dead.

Back again. Eliza. And Eliza. Again and again. Then he stopped. This photograph was different. It was the same pose, the same blood, the same deep slice through her throat, but there was something different about her stare. It dawned on him in horror. She was still alive in this picture.

He flicked back through and the life started the flush in her cheeks. The panic rose in her eyes. She hadn't quite given up on life now. The tears ran down his face. Oh Eliza, I'm sorry I slept through all of this. I could have saved you. The sick bastard who had killed her must have taken his camera. Maybe he had been drugged. Why hadn't he woken up?

Would he see who had killed her? Suddenly the view changed. It was a picture he hadn't taken looking down the empty train carriage. Neither he nor Eliza were in shot.

What the hell was going on?

He looked down at the train tracks. He couldn't stay here. He had to get back to civilisation. He stared at the train tracks. These would have to lead somewhere.

Slipping down from the platform he walked out into the middle of the tracks. It was the best thing he could do, under the current circumstances, he told himself. Putting the camera back into his satchel, he stuffed his hands into his jacket, shivering as the moisture and the deathly chill crept under his clothes. He started down the tracks and into the mist.

Part way down he worried about new trains coming. He wouldn't see them until they were upon him. He stepped out of the middle of the track lines and walked carefully at the side.

Ten minutes later he was stationary, staring in horror. This was the end of the line. Literally. The track stopped with a wooden buffer to take any last movements out of the train. The track hadn't split at any point. He squeezed his eyes shut, trying to think. This was all right. It would be one of those stations you had to go in and out of along the same piece of line. It was obviously a request stop, some god forsaken out of the way place that people rarely wanted to go to.

At least he knew there was only one way to go now.

He walked back to the platform. Nothing had changed. He didn't bother climbing back up. He continued by the side of the train tracks. Lost in the fog. His footsteps crunched loudly against the thick layer of chippings at the side of the track. The only sound in the swirling mass of nothing.

Another ten minutes and he had come to the end of the line. The track stopped, met by another buffer. Beyond that trees started. There had been no junction in the tracks. This was impossible. A sob rose in his throat. His heart pounded against his rib cage.

Calm down.

He took out the digital camera, flicking it on. He would go past the pictures of Eliza, go back to something happy.

The last picture wasn't Eliza.

He was in the photograph, lying on train tracks. His right arm was pulled painfully up and around behind his body. It had obviously been dislocated. Blood splatters everywhere. His mouth a red gaping hole. He looked dead.

David screamed into the mist.

He walked back to the platform, wiping his nose on his sleeve, sobbing without shame. He pulled himself onto the platform. Stopped crying. Folded his legs under himself and sat quietly. Put the camera away. There was nothing else to do.

Half an hour later an empty train pulled up at the platform. It stopped, and the carriage doors hissed open. David looked up at the train. The empty carriage regarded him.

There really wasn't anything else to do.

He got onto the train.

Beryl was acutely aware of the five sheets of slightly crumpled white paper lying on the bar by Noel's elbow. The black type, font size 12, crammed into the sheets, lines of words pushing up against one another. It wasn't possible to read it from a distance, but if someone were to come up to the bar and cast an eye in that direction, they could experience page one of her short story. She felt particularly self-conscious; half-convinced Noel was only saying he liked it in order to be nice to her.

"It reminds me of the old compilations I used to read. You could pick them up for pennies second hand," he was saying, his panama hat slipped slightly to one side. It still looked like he hadn't brushed his hair yet this week. "Marvellous things, collections of ghost stories and horror – the most god-awful melodramatic illustrations on the cover. You'd think the artist had been up all night watching blood-thirsty video nasties and had forgotten to read the damn stories. But I'll tell you this now," he wagged a finger at her. "Artists, illustrators, they don't read the books. They get a vague brief from the art department and draw any old shit. You should have seen some of the first covers they suggested for *Fishbowl*."

Beryl felt he was wandering from the point. "So you read a lot of trashy horror in your youth?" Is this what he thought her writing amounted to?

"No, this is my point," Noel continued. "You'd start reading the stories and realise they were well-written, clever plots, genuinely creepy. Good British creepy tales of terror, decent, upstanding types writing short stories. It was all the rage at one point. We did well in our horror back then." He stopped, as if the lecture was finished, and leant back a little. "Of course, that was then and this is now, and this isn't in vogue as much. If you're going to write short stories, you want to be profound but suitably vague at the same time, end it half way through without conclusion, have at least one depressive in there who's painting the walls with materials of suspicious origins; either that or depravity with drug abuse and society ills." He waved a hand at her writing. "We don't want to be scared these days, we want to be depressed."

"So you don't think it's any good?" She felt deflated.

"I'm not talking about whether it's any good. I'm talking about publishing, which has nothing to do with good writing. Now, if you're going to write a novel, you might want to think about crime. Crime sells. Especially from Scandinavia at the moment. I wonder why it is. Maybe it's a lack of sunshine; maybe it's the depression. Either that or you want to write something that can be heavily merchandised, if you know what I mean."

"Not really."

"Children's toys," he explained, his eyes wide.

"That's not really why I write."

"Me neither," he sympathised. "I am just trying to impress upon you the nature of modern publishing, should you ever get any such notions. Because you will not get rich. Very few succeed." Only Noel Farthing, the one-hit-wonder with his fishbowls who was struggling to think of anything more to say to the world, he thought, a little sourly. And here was this young, slightly naive girl who was probably churning out one of these tales a night, purely for fun and not worrying that half the world was judging her on her words and wanting to know what would come next. "Have you ever thought about a blog?"

"Sorry?"

"A writing blog. I hear a lot of writers use that medium."

"I don't really like reading online."

"Too right," Noel agreed, finishing his cocktail. "Give me a paperback I can hold in my hand any day. Pages that soak up the grease from your fingers and yellow on the windowsill. Books that travel in your bag. Something physical."

Beryl crossed her arms on the bar and looked into the ice cubes in her drink. This wasn't quite what she'd been expecting from showing Noel Farthing, *the* Noel Farthing, some of her work, although she didn't know what she had wanted.

"I know; I suggest a writing project," Noel burst out.

"I wasn't really looking for homework."

"Write me five hundred words on Darcy McMorris, a whisky distillery technician living on the Isle of Mann who believes in fairies and doesn't eat red meat." Damn, he thought to himself, that's the best idea I've had all week and I've just given it away.

Beryl gazed idly out of the window. Adrien walked along the path outside the hotel at the seafront in Portmeirion. She almost waved to him as he glanced into the bar, wanted to thank him for rescuing her from the tides. But that had all been a dream, and the pleasant Rufus-Adrien existed in her head, whilst the aloof alter-ego was already passing by. She looked back at Noel. "Shall I give you the start of a story?"

He brightened at this, having seen the moody gardener as well. "Gladly."

"Tell me a story about a Welsh woman."

"Any particular one?"

"Let's call her Ffion."

"Ffion?"

"Ffion Owen," she paused. "I mentioned her name the other evening on the boat and I felt I'd put my foot in it."

"You had," Noel confirmed.

"But I'd just read the name out of a guidebook. I hadn't meant any harm."

"Oh, my dear, don't you worry yourself about that," he petted her hand. "We needn't worry ourselves about the staff. And a rather arsey bunch at that. And there's no reason why Ffion's name shouldn't be mentioned, she was a very nice girl."

"Was a very nice girl?"

Noel shrugged. "Probably still is, but I haven't seen her for a lot of years. She used to work here. I knew her then of course. Lord, it must be fifteen years ago now. She worked in the bookshop, and wrote the Welsh sections of that guidebook. A sweet little thing, a blonde Welsh cherub. She would have been about your age at the time. Wouldn't have said boo to a goose."

"Adrien didn't look very happy that I'd mentioned her."

"No, but that man is an arsehole, and the sooner you realise it, the better," Noel said, suddenly quite aggressive. "He had a summer job in the gardens after his A-levels when Ffion was working here, so they would have been colleagues."

"So what happened? Did she steal the family silver and run off in the night."

"Quite the opposite. Ffion was treated very badly by some of the staff, people unfortunately still employed here today. It got to the point that she'd had enough, and she just walked out of her job. I don't blame the girl."

"And travelled the world," Beryl finished for him.

"Yes," Noel looked curious. "How did you know that?"

The postcards. Worry leapt up her throat; she couldn't admit those to anyone. Postcards of longing, love, loneliness, from a woman called Ffion to a man called Huw Dodd. "Just something I heard," she said off hand. "She was involved with that gardener, wasn't she?"

Noel snorted. "You've been hearing a lot more than the odd thing, haven't you? Eavesdropping?" He grinned. "Because you've not got the story quite right. She was never involved with Huw Dodd."

"But..." The tone of the postcards had been quite clear.

"A terrible case of unrequited love I'm afraid. She idolised him, and I am still at a loss to explain why. He wasn't as miserable a turd as he is today, but a girl like Ffion could have done a lot better back then. I suppose love is blind. And Huw scorned her. Treated her with utter disdain, but she ran around his heels like a dumb puppy. In some respects, quite a foolish girl," Noel mused. "But I suppose that's love for you, and unfulfilled is said to be the strongest."

"And she left to get over Huw Dodd."

"That's about it." Noel agreed. "And she must have done it, because I've never seen her since."

She had been writing him postcards for years, and she wasn't getting over him. Beryl felt a sudden desire to go back to her flat and read through all the postcards, catalogue them by date to see just how long it had been going on. "And what about Huw; did he move on?"

"The term unrequited love suggests a one way street. But I wonder if he's repressed." Noel lent forward, the look of gossip on his face. "Huw was estranged from his wife when all this happened, and they got divorced shortly afterwards. He treated Ffion terribly, but it does make one wonder if there isn't some truth in the saying, that there's a thin line between love and hate. And there must have been something, because the mere mortals that we are, are not allowed to mention her name in Huw's presence."

"So if Adrien had worked here back then, he must have known something of what happened," Beryl said to herself, considering why Adrien had seemed defensive that evening.

"Oh yes," Noel agreed. "He'll probably know a lot more than I do, having worked with Huw. And he was here at the end, when Ffion walked out on her job, her home and everyone. He'd have been here to witness the fall out."

Bluebells still flowered in the woodlands. Beryl paused, casting her eyes across the spread of forest. This track seemed to have been cut out of the earth, a channel for pedestrians to follow; tree roots and layers of Welsh slate chippings poking out from the side of the channel. In the branches overhead a blackbird chattered to anyone who cared to listen.

She'd been in Wales over two weeks and this was the first time she had left the sanctuary of Portmeirion. Once settled in her flat, she hadn't felt inclined to leave the comfort zone. The few safe roads of the village, a supermarket delivery truck that would deliver everything required. No job to worry about, no telephone calls to disturb. She could sleep late, stay up till the small hours of the night, wander with no purpose and send postcards to her mother – no landline and the mobile phone battery had long since run down and had not been recharged. There were afternoons to sit and discuss nonsense with Noel, under the pretence that they were involved in serious literary investigations. Cerys was trying to teach her a few words of Welsh, and promising to find a 'teach-yourself' book she'd once bought for an old boyfriend who'd quickly lost interest when he realised there would be effort involved. She'd read all the books she'd brought from home; written the short stories roaming her mind; and sat on the balcony and day-dreamed for hours to music.

Now she was widening her horizons, walking out to the next town. Portmeirion was built on the south side of a hilly outlet into the estuary. Up and over the hill, the little track came down near smoke-encrusted engineering sheds belonging to the narrow gauge railway that ran up into the hills, the beginning of the Snowdonia National Park. Far beyond sight, there were mountains and mists. Welsh slate, rain-battered scree, legends and tales. More imminent was the cob, a man-made embankment that ran across another section of the estuary, with road and narrow gauge railway heading in a straight line to the small town of Porthmadog.

It was a popular tourist attraction for the railway, the harbour with the expensive yachts, and the fine beaches beyond, running around to the picturesque village cove of Borth-y-Gest. Beryl crossed over the cob beside the narrow gauge railway, stepping up to the old-fashioned platform and train station. A few tourists had gathered early, waiting for the next departure to the hills. Beryl walked out of the station, over the bridge and into town. The centre of the Porthmadog was reasonably busy, filled with the usual line up of banks, tourist-tat shops and chain branches. Here and there signs of the recession hung glumly between their better-off brothers: a boarded up pub with cheap plywood nailed over the windows. For sale signs on the flats above shops. An empty cavern where a business had failed and now the space was for dust and unwanted mail that no one would open. Beyond the main road there were lines of pebble-dashed terraced homes that looked grey and saddened when the sun didn't shine.

She did the run of the charity shops – for there was always second hand, and these days it was something of a booming trade. Flicking through the books for something new to read. Tatty crumbled spines, dedications to friends and family as books were given and then discarded into the next charity bag, sometimes never even read. Bookshelves were cleared for new volumes, emptied for a move or a death, or simply in the knowledge that the book would never be read again. She found a couple of compilations of ghost stories printed in the seventies that Noel had talked of. At twenty pence each, she hardly felt as though she could leave them. Her shoulder bag was soon full of second hand books, each with a history and a story of its own.

The afternoon was conducted at Borth-y-Gest, a little village just around the headland from Porthmadog. A small bay swept in a horseshoe form, a line of terraced houses, facades of white, green and blue, looking back out to sea. The road followed the natural curve of the coastline before petering out to a dead end with a gravelled footpath continuing past wind-whipped benches and an old Second World War bunker barely clinging on to the cliff side. Beryl had taken a path that led down to the sands, dark jagged rocks emerging from the grains like windbreakers. She'd sat on the beach, her attention alternating from a book to the incoming tide.

Putting the collection of short stories aside, now finished, she lay on the beach and stared up at the sky, white clouds passing over head. The book had been a collection of short ghostly tales from the seventies, no better or worse than her own efforts. But it wasn't the kind of book she could imagine being published today with major success. Certainly not something she could recall having seen in the bookshops when she was looking for ideas of new reading material.

Noel was right; this kind of thing simply wasn't in vogue in publishing at the moment. Not that she exclusively wrote short horror fiction, but accepting how the writing world actually was today was a reality kick for her. At the end of her stay in Portmeirion it would be back to the flat share and the office temping till she could secure a new permanent job. Blandness and mindlessness, to the point of ticking off days until retirement. It didn't really seem like the way to live. Just waiting for the end so she didn't have to bother anymore.

It wasn't until she'd wandered back into Porthmadog and was heading down the high street towards the cob that was she knocked out of her melancholic chain of thoughts.

"Beryl!"

Dafydd, the slightly rounded, young ruddy cheeked gardener, was waving as he marched up the footpath in her direction. "Come to the pub with me, now."

"Oh, no, thanks." She faltered as Dafydd rushed up to her, clearly ignoring what she was saying. "I was going to head back."

"No, come with me," he said, turning her back to the town. "I'm going to the pub. I said I'd have a pint with Adrien but I don't think I can be doing with it. Talking about bloody work. If you're there, we'll have to change the subject."

Beryl grimaced as she was frog marched to a pub that had seen better days. She, Dafydd and Adrien sat in a pub together did not sound appealing. The third unwanted wheel. But she was pushed in through the doorway and it was too late. She could see Adrien ahead, solitary at a table with a pint of beer. It didn't seem to fit the mental image she'd built of him – he seemed too sophisticated for such working class pleasures. He ought to be at a cocktail bar where the drinks cost more than she earned in a week, and people gazed at one another through drooping eyes, making ever-so witty comments.

"Adrien!" Dafydd almost roared, waking his colleague out of his thoughts. "Look who I bumped into down the road. Said you'd give her a lift back to the village."

She looked around at Dafydd. "No, I..."

"Don't mind, do you?" Dafydd continued. "Anyway, I'm off for a quick whizz and then we'll get the drinks in. Don't worry, Beryl, I'll get you something local to try."

And with that Beryl and Adrien were left alone. She glanced around the pub – decoration that was at least a decade too old, worn-out tables that were scratched and stained to oblivion. She hooked her fingers through the straps of her shoulder bag, feeling distinctly out of place. Nodded to him. "Hello, Rufus."

"Rufus?"

Oh Christ, she thought, that had been the dream. "Sorry, Adrien."

He raised his eyebrows, indulging in a private thought. It was hard to say whether he was insulted by the fact she had forgotten his name, or amused that she had been under the impression he was called Rufus. "Are you going to sit down?"

She felt like a small child. She wasn't sure what it was exactly, but Adrien made her feel diminutive without doing anything. Beryl sat down opposite him, setting her bag of books on her knee, and wished Dafydd would hurry up.

"You've been buying books today?"

Beryl looked down at the bag, the book on top with a particularly trashy front cover. "Yes. I looked round the charity shops here. I've read everything I brought."

"For the extended holiday."

She looked up sharply. Another dig?

"I hear that it's not actually self-financed."

"What isn't?"

"Not that it's my business really," Adrien continued, "but that you have an eccentric relative who likes to give inappropriate gifts."

Beryl wondered just how much the gardeners had been gossiping about her on a morning whilst they all took breakfast."Yes, it's my aunt. But this time it was quite a good idea. I think I needed a break from all the temping."

"You're just temping at the moment? Office work?"

"Yes, well, until I can get something permanent. I was made redundant from my last permanent job."

"And you like reading?"

"Yes, I read a lot." This was like being at an interview. Beryl watched him arch his fingers on the table top.

"Fiction?"

"Mostly."

"Have you picked up a copy of Noel's book to read, then?"

She smiled weakly. There was a distinct sound of distaste in his voice now that he spoke of Noel. "I think everyone's already read *Fishbowl*. Surely even you have."

Adrien smiled wryly, relenting in the interrogation. "Between you and me, yes, I have. But don't tell Noel that. He doesn't need any more encouragement." He paused, looking across at her, unashamedly holding her gaze as if they were about to declare a staring war. "Did you know Noel from elsewhere?"

"No," she shook her head. "He just sort of... accosted me. Started talking to me."

"He does that a lot." Adrien commented. "You could be forgiven for thinking he was avoiding writing."

"Three cheers for three of the local brew." Dafydd rejoined them, three pint glasses clinking, miraculously held together by one man without unsettling the head on any one of the drinks. He set the pints down upon the table. "You'll be all right driving back after two pints, won't you?" he asked Adrien. "Because Beryl here needs a lift home, she's a sack of books with her, see. And I won't be heading back to the village till tomorrow, 'cause I live over here in Porthmadog, like, and this evening I intend to get pissed, so I won't be driving anyone anywhere."

"After that very articulate argument, I shall have to drive the lady home."

Beryl peered into the murky malted depths of the pint Dafydd had brought her. It wasn't exactly a girl's drink, and she wasn't a beer drinker.

"Adrien lives in the village, you see," Dafydd told her.

"You get a house with the job?"

Adrien nodded.

"Head gardener's cottage," Dafydd added.

Beryl coughed at the information and the intensely strong malted flavour of the ale. "Head gardener? I thought that was Huw Dodd."

"Don't mention his name to me tonight. Sour old ball sac." Dafydd cleared half a pint in one draught. "Was on my bloody case all day today. About bedders, you know, bedding plants. And at the end of the day, it doesn't look that bad. Most of the visitors don't even know what they're looking at anyway."

Beryl was only listening to Dafydd with half an ear, more concerned with the politics of the village. "How did you manage to get the cottage?"

"It was empty," Adrien shrugged. "They prefer it lived in. And Huw doesn't care to live in the village. He lives in..."

"Bryn Bwbach," Beryl finished off handed without thinking, her pronunciation a little off kilter, but it was close enough for the two gardeners to understand.

Adrien was intrigued. "How do you know that?"

She was about to point out that it was the address on the postcards, when she realised that no one knew about the postcards, or certainly at the very least, no one knew that she had them in her flat. Just like the dream a few nights ago, it was one of those things she ought to plead ignorance to in the light of day. "Oh," she shook her head, trying to think of a plausible explanation. "I must have heard it somewhere. Maybe Cerys mentioned it."

"She does like to talk," Dafydd concurred. "You'll know more about the place than I do by the end of your stay."

They stayed for as long as it took Adrien to drink the pint and a half he'd been left with. Progress sped up considerably when a couple of Daffyd's friends rolled up, leaving Adrien by age and Beryl by language as outsiders in the group. They'd left the pub together, Beryl hurrying beside Adrien's solid march up a side road to his parked car. The drive back to the village wasn't actually that long, but it felt like an age: polite chit chat and vagueness, Adrien's attention drifting to somewhere beyond present company and Beryl worrying that once again she was proving to be intellectually unstimulating company.

The head gardeners' cottage wasn't actually in the village per see, certainly not the ticketed section, but it lay in the wider grounds, as did the Castle where Beryl had first checked in. Adrien had driven her down to the entrance gates to the central village, her holiday home only a couple of hundred meters walk from there. As he'd stopped by the gates, the engine idling, he'd looked pensive, on the verge of asking her something, then changing his mind and retreating back into his thoughts. "Good night."

Beryl smiled politely, opening the car door and stepping out. "Thank you for the lift." She paused in pushing the door too, looking back into the interior of the vehicle. He really was such an oddity. He looked thoughtful, relaxed, very open to the world and yet of all the staff she had met, he was the one she didn't really know where she stood with. Even Huw Dodd left no ambiguity, making it clear that he hated her along with most other people on planet earth. Probably even himself. "Be seeing you."

Adrien smiled to himself. "This place is getting to you."

She stood and watched as he reversed the car around to drive back up the road. More than you'd know, she thought quietly, before heading back to her temporary home.

A wooden spoon hung by the door like an alternative bell pull or door knocker. It was a large, intricately carved spoon, polished and smoothed to fine detail, with a wheel worked into the design of the handle.

"You must be the new music teacher, Beryl Cerys."

Beryl turned from the front entrance to the Seagull Inn, an image of tailored professionalism in an indigo blue embroidered Victorian jacket and long skirts, a neat satchel of papers in her hand. The stupid straw bonnet was gone, left upstairs in her lodgings, and instead her hair was piled artistically on her head, a swirl of curls and curves. Beryl had no idea how she had managed it, but such technicalities weren't important in dreams.

Noel approached, dressed in black, sweeping robes as if he were an academic. "Maximus," he introduced himself. "I am the village elder, and very charmed to make your acquaintance." He stooped forward, taking her hand and rather theatrically kissing it. "And how are you finding our modest little hamlet?"

"I am finding it very well, thank you."

"I would gladly show you the best features of the area," Maximus (Noel) continued, a little territorially taking her by the elbow to lead her away from the inn.

"Thank you, but I have a prior engagement." Sternly, but to the point, Beryl pushed his grabbing hands away. "I have my first pupil to teach, and I mustn't be late."

"Then let me walk you..."

"No, I do not want to interrupt your original purpose." Beryl hurried away, down a side street, eager to get out of his immediate vicinity. There had been something distinctly lecherous about this Maximus (Noel). Something that left her ill at ease.

Down the little wynd, there was a particular stone building that stole focus away from all of its neighbours. It had a well-built, classical facade, lines of columns up between every window, and at the double doorway, a Grecian woman on either side to replace the column, her hands above her head to keep the plinth in place. Robes full of curves and drapes; it was amazing the realistic quality a skilled mason could recreate in rock. Her attention was drawn to the entrance itself and the object hanging from the wall at the side. Beryl stepped up to the door. It was another wooden spoon. This was a particularly large spoon, with two hands at the top of the spoon head, a dozen hearts tumbling down into the hands, which formed the handle. This spoon didn't look as though it received much care, left out in all weathers, for the wood looked brittle and was cracking.

"This must be the new girl," a woman's voice commented.

"I don't think we need to worry. She doesn't look like serious competition."

Beryl glanced down the wynd, but she was the only person in the lane.

"Not the brightest perhaps."

She stepped back out of the shadows of the town house and into the bright sunlight. "I suggest you show yourselves."

The women tittered. "Definitely not bright."

"We're hardly hiding from you."

She looked back to the building's facade, and one of the Greek women winked at her. The other took her hands away from the plinth, which was more than capable of holding itself up. Leaning forward, she looked Beryl in the eye. "You're the one they call Beryl Cerys? The town elder's spoken of you. He lives in here."

"I should go."

"Why? Do I intimidate you?"

"Get back!" The other woman hissed. "There are others coming."

The woman pulled back into position. Beryl looked up the lane as Kev and Dafydd – or whatever they were calling themselves in this place – strolled towards her, fishing nets slung over their shoulders. They were chattering and joking, bowlegged as they sauntered up to her, giving her a saucy nod before whistling at Maximus' house. "Morning ladies!"

She looked back to the Grecian woman, returned to a stance of lifeless statues although one of the women had pulled down her top to expose her ample bosom.

"Always a nice view down this way."

They rounded the corner and disappeared from view. Flickerings of life again. The woman on the right pulled her neckline up to the vicinity of her neck. "Weren't you on your way to teach a music lesson?" she asked Beryl.

"How did you..."

"We know everything," the other woman spoke, for the first time meeting Beryl's eye. "You'd better get a move on."

Time sped up and slowed down again. There was a music lesson conducted in a cottage, but with amnesia, she had already forgotten where the cottage was or what the child was called by the time she was walking back through a wood towards the village. Bluebells grew through the glade, a purple carpet of dappled light. The sound of the sea rustled through the leaves. The woodland path gently wound down towards the village and sea level. Beryl near-skipped down the track, elated as she was, swinging her satchel full of sheet music beside her, humming an idle tune.

At the crescendo she spun around in the middle of the track, savouring the feeling of her heavy skirts pirouetting around her legs. Arms outstretched gracefully, a moment of faltering as the satchel hit a tree trunk, releasing the catch and spraying a semi circle of papers across the forest.

Her arms dropped, the bubble burst, and Beryl gazed across the forest ground, ashen faced. "Oh no," she moaned to herself, wondering how she would get the sheets back into order. She ought to remember her age and not go skipping down country lanes as if she were a mere child.

Dropping to a crouch, she started to gather up the papers. Hoping the breeze would not pick up. She heard footsteps increase in tempo down the track. "Did you have an accident?"

Beryl glanced up, feeling a lock of hair loosen from the style and drop over her face. "No," she said as she watched Rufus (Adrien) pick up the few remaining papers for her. "Just a lack of concentration," she added, brushing her loose hair behind her ear.

"No damage done."

Beryl stood up as he approached, accepting the papers. "Thank you. You're very kind."

"I only do what any other would..."

"I don't think so," she halted him, rather forwardly putting a hand to his wrist, as if words were actions. "I am very grateful for what you did on my first day in the village. I'm not certain everyone would have taken a stranger into their home. I knew nothing of the tide then."

He smiled, perhaps a little embarrassed by the intensity. "But you know of the tide now."

"Know of and know of. I know that I must make sure I am safe daily when the tide comes. But I still find it strange. I'd never lived by the sea before. I hadn't known it was such a threat. I suppose all people who dwell on the coast are used to this."

"It's only our village that suffers."

"This doesn't happen anywhere else?"

"Only here," he assured her as they fell into step with one another along the track. "Our village is caught between the two kings, so most days the tide comes. But you will have heard the stories by now."

"I can assure you I've been told nothing."

"Really?"

"Would you tell me? It's not a secret is it?"

Rufus (Adrien) laughed. "It's no secret, but it's been happening for so long now that people rarely think of it. It's like the sun rising and sinking every day. Outside of our hamlet no one is particularly interested in what happens, and I doubt the kings really think of it now. And we, the innocent parties are trapped between the pull and push of the two."

He was talking in riddles, Beryl thought. "The village has two kings?"

He smiled lightly. "Of sorts, but neither king is in the village." He paused as they came to a downward curve in the track. "You'll see from here," he told her, diverging from the main track and following a narrow path through the trees to a seat near the cliff. The view was particularly fine, over the broiling waves of the ocean, over the top of the village and up over to the cliffs beyond. "Do you see the mansion house in the distance?"

Beryl stepped up beside him, peering over the landscape. On the cliffs at the far side of the village, high above the reach of the daily tidal surge was a fine, proudly isolated manor house set at the edge of the plains. She had seen this building when she had first arrived here, waking up in the hills high above the village. "I see it."

"Savant lives there. They say he's not left the building these past fifteen years. He sits in his palace and watches the sea. And his brother, Nevent, lives over there." He waved his hand out towards the sea and Beryl assumed he meant that the other king lived on a boat. Perhaps a luxury liner. "They once were very close, but they have not spoken or set eyes upon one another for fifteen years. Our village is caught between the two."

"What has this got to do with the tide?"

"It's Nevent who pushes the tide up every day. He is trying to wash his brother away, but he never has the strength to get up the cliffs. Fifteen years he has been doing this, and still he tries every day. He must realise that he'll never get to the top."

"So the tides are due to a fifteen-year-old feud between two brothers," Beryl concluded. At any other time she might have scoffed at such an idea. But this was a place where magical things were possible. She had seen the mermaids from her window when high tide was upon the village and she was safely locked up in a watertighted room, as the inventions were referred to. Her gaze drifted to the village by the shore. Suffering in the middle of a feud that was presumably nothing to do with them. She looked back to Rufus (Adrien). "If this has been happening for so long, why haven't you all moved to somewhere more peaceful?"

He smiled at her, as if she had a lot to learn. "People do a lot of strange things out of habit. Sometimes we can't help ourselves."

Beryl was still pondering the matter that evening in Arabella (Cerys)'s parlour. The tide that day was due for the evening, a short sharp snap, quickly up and down in a couple of hours. It was too early to retire to her room, and she felt in need of company. In truth, what Rufus (Adrien) had told her had left her with only more questions. Whilst coming to light, the arrangements in this curious little village were still distinctly hazy.

"Of course, whilst he continues to consider wool in such terms, he ought not to be surprised that we invite competition," Arabella (Cerys) said to the merchant who accompanied her by the fire. She was neatly curled in a wide armchair, long wooden knitting needles clicking together as she worked on a woollen item of indescribable proportions. The merchant, a stocky, pink-faced man with a Quaker's hat, lent forward from his wooden stool, warming his hands at the fire. Beryl was sat the edge of the room, close to the window. She had a small book with her, which lay open on the round table, but she couldn't concentrate, and spent her time flicking between the darkening inky view from the window, and the chatter by the illumination of the fire.

"Can you see the water yet from the window, Miss Cerys?" Arabella (Cerys) asked.

Beryl looked back to the window. "It's just appearing at the corner of the square.

Arabella (Cerys) set her knitting down in her lap and looked back to the merchant. "I had better lock the doors," she said to him, "or else we are all sure to be drowned!" she laughed the final comment as if drowning was no more than an inconvenience. As she stood up, they heard a loud clatter from the bar outside – an un-watertighted area, the first room in the inn, and assumedly empty of all life by now. People ought to be ready in their safe rooms. There was a knock at the parlour room door. The three occupants stared at each other, a little horrified that there was an unknown on the other side.

Not one to let anything frighten her into submission, Arabella (Cerys) stood up and answered the door. "Why, Rufus!" she exclaimed as she pulled back the door to reveal Rufus (Adrien) stood on the threshold with a basket of logs. "What are you doing here at this time? You'll not get back to your cottage now; you know. Your cottage level is lower that the inn's."

"I know, I have left it late, but you'd ordered firewood."

"Firewood that could have waited till tomorrow," she added. "Will you join us?" she added, a pointless question now as he had few alternatives. Passing him, she hurried through the bar to lock the front door. A puddle of seawater was rapidly growing across the bar floor. Throwing the latch over, she hurried back and heaved the parlour's watertight door into place. The merchant got up from his stool and helped her to get the wheel into position. Rufus (Adrien) emptied the logs into a wrought-iron basket by the fire, before straightening and scanning over the available seating in the room. He selected a chair to the edge, close to the side table where Beryl sat.

"Miss Beryl," he nodded to her. "I had not expected to see you so soon again after this afternoon."

Beryl caught Arabella (Cerys)'s expression from her peripheral view. A knowing smile. This was all more expected than unexpected. "I bumped into Rufus this afternoon," she announced, louder than was really necessary, and although speaking for Arabella (Cerys)'s benefit, she had her eyes focused on Rufus all the time. "He was kind enough to tell me about the two kings. I hadn't realised why these tides occurred every day until now."

"Oh Nevent and Savant," Arabella (Cerys) groaned. She returned to her armchair and her knitting. "They are the reason we suffer under this curse. And there is no longer any common ground for them to meet, so I don't suppose this will ever end. And to think they used to be so close. I remember when I was but a girl, such harmonious times. And now this feud."

"So they used to be close?"

"Incredibly so."

"What happened to push them apart?"

"Oh, the usual," Arabella (Cerys) said. "A woman. Albeit a very special woman, but at the end of the day, just a woman. She moved to the area. A graceful, slender, very beautiful woman. Captivating, I suppose you might say. The kind of woman you just wanted to hate because she was too perfect in every way; yet she was the definition of generosity and kindness – all womenfolk admired her greatly. She was too perfect for this world. I suppose it was her undoing really. If only she'd had a little harshness."

"If she'd said no," the merchant agreed.

"Exactly," the landlady nodded her confirmation. "At least to one of them, although that could have left the village with just as many problems. But if she'd been direct with them both at the beginning then they might not have become so obsessed."

"But even if she had told the brothers on the day she arrived in the village, that she would never marry either, I doubt that would have protected them for falling for the lady," the merchant pointed out, becoming quite animated as he recalled the lovely lady. He had only been coming to the village on trading missions a couple of summers before her arrival.

"It was a tragedy waiting to happen," Arabella (Cerys) concluded. "You can work the story out for yourself," she continued, looking pointedly at Beryl. "Nevent and Savant fell head over heels in love with her. It turned into a terrible rivalry. She didn't want to marry either of them. But she liked both, considered both as friends. Oh but the fighting that it all resulted in. Then the brothers stopped speaking and went their separate ways, Savant to the cliffs, Nevent to the sea. Each one trying to best the other, become the better man. And so we've been here the last fifteen years, and no doubt the next fifteen to come."

"And what happened to the lady?"

"Which lady?"

"That the brothers loved."

"Oh, she's all forgotten now. All they focus on is the feud."

"But where is she?"

Arabella (Cerys) set down her knitting, and leant back in her armchair to mull over the question. "Honest truth is, I don't know. She's not been heard of many a year. Do you know, Rufus?"

"No," he admitted. "I think she became lost in the story. The feud took over; it's all the brothers think about. She disappeared the same night they went their separate ways." He looked directly at Beryl. "It's an astute question, because I don't think anyone's given her a thought since."

Beryl found she was blushing and looked down at her unread book. "And the village has been plagued by the tides ever since."

"That's exactly it," Arabella (Cerys) said. "And so it will be until someone talks some sense into the brothers, although there's no one who could do that now. So I suppose we'll just have to wait until they pass on into the next life." She paused, looking into the fire. "But the intensity of that feud will keep them going far longer than any of us will last."

Cerys fanned herself with one of the cards and pressed the patch of back between her shoulder blades against the cool plaster of the wall. They were entering a hot snap, heat wave, the winds having dropped leaving the people on the ground to experience sweltering heat before the height of summer was ready to take it. She was glad she'd finished her shift at twelve o'clock noon. There was little fun to be found in working in this kind of heat – she may almost have said it was better than working in the rain, but rain would have been blissful in this heat; and besides which, Cerys was a Welshwoman born and bred on the slopes of Snowdonia. Rain she could cope with.

Beryl was on the floor on the opposite side of the living room, flicking through the small hardback dictionary Cerys had brought. She too was lent against the wall, in-between a fire extinguisher and the open doorway out onto the balcony. She had one bare leg stretched out into the rectangle of sunlight on the carpet, her toes unconsciously wiggling as she searched for something in the dictionary. She looked up at Cerys. "Haul."

"Haul what where?"

"No," she held up the dictionary. "I'm speaking Welsh."

"Oh, *haul*," Cerys repeated, getting the accent right. Sun. "Yes, there's plenty of that today. I just can't concentrate on the lesson since seeing this," she held up the postcard she'd been cooling the sweat on her forehead with. "Is this for real? And you've got a whole bag full of them?"

Beryl grimaced. She hadn't intended on sharing the discovery with anyone, certainly not anyone connected with Portmeirion or Huw Dodd's circle of acquaintance. These intensely personal postcards, detailing one side of a relationship continued for the past decade, assumedly one that hadn't been consummated in any way, because people said that Huw Dodd never set foot outside of Wales. Cerys had come over to her flat this afternoon intending to give a short Welsh lesson. The bag had been on the coffee table, and Cerys had happened to glance inside. The more Beryl wished Cerys would return her attention to the dated, second-hand Welsh textbooks, the more she looked at the bag of postcards until temptation had been too much. "I found the bag at the train station."

"When you arrived at Porthmadog?"

"No, in Shrewsbury."

"Shrewsbury?" Cerys pursed her lips. "What would they be doing in Shrewsbury? That's not even in Wales. Huw's not left Wales for years."

"They were in the ladies."

"Bloody hell." Cerys' eyes were goggling now. "This must be the find of the year. I don't get how they ended up in a public toilet in England. And there's a bagful of these things, all from the same person? Ffion? I never met her; that happened way before I came here to work. But she left well over ten years ago and she's never been back since. We're not supposed to talk about her in Huw's presence. I just thought it was because the joke had worn thin, people winding him up the wrong way, you know what I mean? But they've actually been in touch all these years." She looked down at the handwritten side of the postcard she was holding. "This one is five years old." She flipped it over. It was a view of Auckland, New Zealand. She smiled wryly. "Almost like something we could have in the village here," she commented. "What does it say on the back? It's Mission Bay. This fountain with the overweight seahorses could fit in here quite nicely."

"There's postcards from all over the world in there," Beryl said, nodding to the paper carrier bag still on the coffee table. If only she'd remembered to put it away last night, back into the kitchen cupboard, beside the rubbish bin. Out of sight, away from eyes of visitors. Away from questions.

"She's really been living it up since she left here."

"She must have covered pretty much every continent now. She could write travel guides to the world. Just imagine the experiences she must have had. These postcards will barely touch the surface."

"Yes, but it's sad really. She's messed up. Not really living."

"She's travelled the world!"

"And she's still simpering after Huw Dodd. Huw Dodd of all people!" Cerys slapped the New Zealand postcard down on the coffee table and dibbled in the paper bag for fresh reading material. "What is it now: ten, fifteen years since she left this place? And she's still not over him; she's still sending him postcards to let him know where she is and that she's thinking of him. She's not really moving on with her life, is she? Just imagine some of the men she must have met. The opportunities she'll have missed. And yet all she wants is Huw. I don't understand that. He's such a miserable old fart."

"I suppose love is blind."

"What, and absence makes the heart grow fonder?" Cerys didn't sound convinced. "We could quote clichés at each other all afternoon. I just can't understand how someone can be so needy. But then of course, I don't suppose I have experience. I've been out with a few lads, you know, but I don't think I'd particularly miss any of them if I went travelling, you know what I mean? You ever been in love, Beryl? I mean proper gut-wrenching stuff that makes you write postcards for years and years?"

Beryl smiled wistfully. "Not the postcard-writing kind." She'd never had a lot of success in selecting boyfriend material. She'd had her drips, her possessives, her blands and even one with a particularly unpleasant nasty physical temper. Nothing that had ever made her heart go boom, at least not in the romantic sense.

"Maybe it's just that I can't get my head round what Huw's got. He's really not appealing."

"Perhaps he was different back when Ffion was here."

"Maybe," Cerys conceded. "It was a long time ago and neither of us knew him then. Still, it's a bit weird, the whole thing."

Perhaps it was the heat, melting normality, leaving everything hazy as the temperature rose and mirages danced over the tarmac roads. Water that wasn't there. The week was strange, and Beryl didn't quite feel herself. Whether it was the heat, the change of environment and pace, perhaps even the water, or the fact that she was having a lot of long, lucid dreams about a village by the sea, she wasn't sure. But strange things were happening.

Across from the hotel, in a private grassed area – guests in residence only, thank you – there was a round swimming pool, a white tow path running around the turquoise blue reflected base of the pool, metallic handrails dipping into the cooling water, glinting sunlight. A few sun loungers were lined artistically on the lawn, not too many to make it look like a package holiday, nothing to spoil the scenery. Every seat was taken, mostly by people staying at the hotel, baking in the sun. Cheap paperback novels and bottles of tanning lotion lay on crumpled towels. The glare of light reflected off sunglasses lenses, shoulder straps pushed out of the way.

Sweat beaded up out of skin pores, growing, merging to a droplet that twisted down the back of her neck. Stray, wispy hairs that hadn't been caught in the up do were now plastered to her slightly clammy skin. It was only the morning, and already she was baking. Pushing her sunglasses up on top of her head, to remind herself just how glaringly bright it was, Beryl glanced over the browning bodies. She was most definitely English – not designed for sunshine. She was pale in comparison, and in high factor, waterproof sun block, it was a status that wasn't going to change any time soon. She had considered following a successful tactic of the previous three days – hiding in the flat until the evening, lying on the floor reading paperbacks, typing in the laptop or looking through Huw's postcards. She'd seen Noel yesterday evening and he'd talked so much of the pool – *the pool*, as if it were the biggest social sensation this year – that the thought of dipping herself bodily into cold fresh water left her gagging for air.

Surprisingly, it wasn't as popular as she'd feared – currently there was only one couple in the pool, not even swimming (it wasn't really a pool for serious swimming), just bobbing at the edge chatting. Leaving her bag and towel to the side, she untied her wrap dress, shedding it and the sandals and walking up to the water's edge. She felt distinctly self conscious, which was silly because everyone else by the pool was in swim wear, one of the women in a bikini that was barely decent. Beryl's retro bikini meant briefs of a dignified size, virtually a pair of shorts, and a generous halter neck top.

Fingers brushing the metallic hand rail, she dipped her foot into the water, the comforting chill of the water flooding her skin. Blissful. On the other side of the hedging, she saw Adrien walking up from the hotel and past the pool area. Checking his watch, idly glancing over the idle rich, a look on his face that suggested he'd happily set them to ten hours hard labour cracking rocks in the sun if he could. He picked up on Beryl, the idle roaming gaze halting, and he gave her particular attention before meeting her eye, all the time not breaking step as he marched up the side of the pool area. There was something about the moment that reminded her that there was a greater proportion of her body that was naked against what was clothed.

"Beryl!"

Noel's voice broke the sweltering tension. "Jesus," Beryl swore under her breath, swiftly completing the descent into the pool, watching Adrien's retreating figure up towards the centre of the village. Noel strolled into the pool area – no jacket and a shirt not tucked into the waistband of his trousers: the extent of him baring his flesh for the sun. He had ginger in his hair and his complexion, his face already pinked, and half an hour out in the sun would probably cripple him. He had a straw hat and sunglasses on to protect that cultured mind. He stroller out to the edge of the pool. Beryl dipped her shoulders under water, her chin brushing the surface tension of the pool.

"It looks a lot better in there than it is out here," Noel commented, stuffing his hands nonchalantly in his trouser pockets to strike a pose. Wishing he had the gumption to go in the pool, but feeling too self conscious over the girth of his stomach to get any more undressed in public than he already was. He'd never been a slender type, but the last couple of years had seen some particular expansion. He might not have minded so much had it been the usual crowd, but when girls like Beryl casually shed their dresses and walked tauntingly into the pool – he had watched the slow descent unnoticed from the shadow of the hotel – it wasn't so easy to overlook one's own failings.

"What have you been doing with yourself to counteract the heat?"

"Very little." Beryl slowly paddled across to the other side of the pool where Noel stood. She didn't want to shout across the pool, quite aware that the other couple had stopped talking and were pretending that they weren't eavesdropping. She hadn't noticed them around the village before – probably only here for a weekend, and maybe they'd recognised Noel. Looking for a little gossip. "Lazing about at home," she started.

In your underwear, Noel silently added.

"Just reading or writing. Moving very little. It's great in here. I could stay put for the day."

"Days like this, you'd be a fool to do much. I suggest we start a reading circle. We'll all stay at home and sweat and read a book. Then we'll gather at the bar in the evening and discuss."

"I don't know how well thinking goes with the heat. Besides, who else are you going to get? I only know the gardeners, and they don't have the time to read a book a day."

"Why do we need anyone else?"

"Two people hardly make a reading circle."

Depends how supple you are, Noel thought. He wandered around the pool to where Beryl had dropped her dress. He picked up the paperback she'd brought with her. "You sit and soak; I'll read this and catch up with you."

Somehow Noel managed to talk one of the women off her sun lounger and into the pool. He commandeered the seating and started on Beryl's current read, completely ignoring her. Beryl didn't mind too much, there were times when Noel could be irritating, and the silence was welcomed. She hovered in the pool, enjoying the temperature, occasionally lifting her hand from the water to see how wrinkled the underside of her fingers had become. The sun continued to batter down upon the tiny village. Her hair felt hot to touch, almost ready to ignite.

As she was climbing back out of the pool, she saw Dafydd marching down the road towards the hotel, pink faced and sweating, his darkened T-shirt almost moulded onto his body. He did not look his jovial usual self. Picking up her wrap dress, neglecting to dry herself off, she hurried into her clothes, feet slipping into her shoes as she moved away from the pool. Ignoring Noel's questions.

"Dafydd!"

He glanced across, an unconscious action at the sound of his name. He looked irritated, not just from the heat and the labour. And here she came running, the lady of leisure, wet tendrils of hair pasted on the back of her neck, pool water dripping from her, thin steam curling off her shoulders. It was all very easy when you had nothing better to do than lay about reading books all day. Making conversation with the staff as an idle distraction.

"Are you all right?"

"No, I'm not bloody all right," he snapped. "Huw's on a day off, Adrien's buggered off to some planning meeting and I say don't worry, I'll sort out the planting by the lake. I'll take the new gardener to show him what's what. We'll get the job done. Shouldn't have opened my bloody mouth. Don't ever volunteer for nothing – I should remember that."

"Surely it's fixable."

He wasn't listening. "It didn't even look like those bushes needed pulling. I should have stopped there. But I wanted to impress someone so I carried out, and now look at the shit we've dug up. It'll be a big pile of nothing, but that idiot's already starting screaming about it, so I've got to come and make a bloody phone call."

"Phone call about what?"

"It's probably nothing more than someone's old fat pig, if you ask me."

"You mean there's a pig in the gardens?"

"Not in the gardens. The woods."

"Did it get loose from a local farm?"

Dafydd gave her a bored look. "Some local farmer put it there. It's dead, see? We've just dug up a load of old pig bones in the woods. Nothing to get excited about. Except that idiot reckons we've got to report it all and make a big deal. So now I've got to go and make a phone call. I could do without this today."

"Bones? Buried in the woods?"

"Save the dramatics for your creative writing classes."

"You're not accosting one of our guests, are you, Dafydd?" A man, who despite the heat was in a full suit without the slightest sign of wilting, approached them. A definition of neat; he was not even breaking out into a sweat. Beryl recognised him as the manager of the hotel. He asked the question with a smile in the corner of his mouth, not wanting to appear the ogre in front of a young lady. At the same time there was an underlying threat, that the gardener should remember his place. There was a distinct line between the world of relaxation the guests enjoyed, and the busy peddling the staff endured to maintain high standards.

"I was coming to find you," Dafydd turned to the manager. "I've just dug up a dead pig, and we have to ring the police about the bones."

"Perhaps we should discuss this in my office," the manager suggested, angling Dafydd in the direction of the hotel. "I'm sure it's nothing to worry about," he added over his shoulder to Beryl. "A misunderstanding. Please don't let it spoil your day."

Go back to the pool and don't worry your pretty little head about a thing. Beryl took her sunglasses from the top of her head, letting them hang loosely by her side between forefinger and thumb, watching the two men walk away. She could still hear them, but already she was excluded from the conversation, which was continued in Welsh. She had had a few lessons from Cerys now, but aside from pleasantries and would you like a beer, she was incapable of communication. Digging up pig bones in the wood must be covered in a later chapter.

"Anything exciting happening?"

Noel's sudden appearance just by her ear made her jump. Beryl set her sunglasses on before looking at Noel. "Dafydd's just dug up a pig."

"A pig? New way of curing meat?"

"Not exactly."

Beryl didn't see any of the gardeners to speak to for the rest of the day. On her way back to the flat in the afternoon, she caught sight of

Dafydd and Adrien. They were around the back of the main buildings, away from tourist tracks, and never saw her. It was an animated conversation, Dafydd like a sullen, defensive child in his scruffy jeans and sweat-stained T-shirt; Adrien the adult back from the planning meeting, whatever that was, in a suit. Throwback to the architecture days, she wondered. Why had he left that profession to return to gardening anyway?

"I'd said take the section north of the pond, above the bridge!" Adrien said.

"Yeah, but you didn't say which way I should be facing."

"North is north whichever way you're facing!"

Beryl slipped around the corner and hurried up the stone steps to her front door. What was it about doing work in the woods that got people so angry? She'd have to take another walk out there tomorrow when this had all settled, see if she could get a look at these pig bones for herself.

"No, you do not need to just check on the plants down there." The man in a suit – presumably a detective – stood jauntily in the middle of the path, hands in pockets, elbows stuck out at comedy angles to be as big a blockage as possible. "Portmeirion's a damn big site, and I'm sure you can find something else to occupy your time."

Beryl, on tip-toes, slowly reached over to lower a sweeping branch of some shrub that was blocking her view. She'd been out wandering in the woods this morning, hoping to *accidentally* stumble on the pig bones. She'd seen nothing of interest until now, hearing the tense conversation on a footpath the next level down. It was enough to warrant a pause in her morning stroll. Presumably the pig bones were further down that track, well out of sight from her current vantage point.

Adrien stood in front of the detective, a wheelbarrow parked to one side. Trying to sweet talk the police into letting him pass. "You've obviously not met my boss..."

"I haven't, but I'm happy to explain to him why this section is out of bounds for today, if he'd like to drop by."

"Come on, I'm not going to disturb your staff. All this for a dead pig?"

"Dead pig?" the detective repeated. "I thought it was an undetonated bomb from the Second World War."

Adrien raised his eyebrows. "Really?"

"Get on with some work elsewhere," the man snapped. "I'm not telling you anything. Gossip time in the gardener's shed'll have to wait another day."

Adrien's expression darkened, his jaw line taunt, as if angry he'd been mistaken for something he wasn't. As he turned to pick up the wheelbarrow handles, Beryl instinctively lent backwards, letting the shrub branch gently bounce back into position. The last thing she wanted was Adrien knowing she had been spying on him.

Continuing down the track towards the village, she wondered what they were doing in the woods. Noel had said that it would be nothing. The police had a civil duty to investigate every report of anything. At worst it would probably turn out that Dafydd had gone digging in the pet cemetery without realising, and got himself in a panic when old Rover's bones had got up tangled on the fork prongs. But a report of bones in the ground was a report of bones in the ground, and the police would be negligent if they didn't do anything about it.

She slowed down as the track approached the end of a tarmac road, watching Adrien march past, pushing the wheelbarrow as though he was ferrying a casualty to A&E. He weaved his way between the few cars that were cluttered ahead – presumably the police's vehicles.

Stumbling down onto the tarmac, she peered down the forest track from where Adrien had come. Did she dare to try her chances there? At least she didn't look like one of the staff; she could plead ignorance – just a tourist exploring the property.

"Are you on a treasure hunt as well?"

There was a man leant against the open boot of a car smoking a cigarette. He was distinctly thin, not a scrap of meat on him, his red curly hair having far more body. His white overalls were unzipped to the waist, and he'd wriggled out of the sleeves to reveal a grey T-shirt advertising a rock concert long since past. He took his attention away from the curl of translucent smoke and onto the girl in the red polka dot sun dress. She didn't look as though she was one of the gardeners – she certainly wasn't dressed for the occasion. If not a gardener, then a paying guest? It was a bit early for the day trippers to have already been strolling through the woods.

"Excuse me?"

He smiled wryly, dropping the end of the cigarette and stubbing it out under his foot. "We've had a couple of gardeners by wanting to *get on with their work*. I must say, I'm very impressed by how industrious the staff here are. Although I don't think you work here, do you?"

She shook her head.

"Tourist?"

"Something like that."

"Well, I can hear you don't come from around here. English; same as me."

"And what are you?"

"Me? Just a bloke having a fag."

"I meant are you a tourist?"

He grinned. "I'm an archeozoologist. Over from Bangor University. Here in a professional capacity."

"You're a student."

"Christ no, I'm a lecturer." He paused, considering her. "We're both being very coy. You're out in the woods trying to find out what the police are up to. I'm out here helping the police, just taking a break. I've watched the gardeners ever so casually saunter down there, and then march back in filthy moods. I could have told them what they wanted to know, but I couldn't be bothered. And then you just strolled out of the undergrowth, and I'm intrigued. Because the village has only been open half an hour, and there's no way even the most energetic of tourists could have managed to stroll around the woods and come back out already."

"I'm staying on site."

"Ah," he nodded. "I suppose you'll have heard the gossip then?"

"I heard something about pig bones, but I don't know if it's true. Are you here to dig?"

"I really shouldn't be talking to you." He heard himself saying the sentence, and he knew that he really shouldn't be talking to her, because this was the start of a police investigation. It would be in the papers in a few days' time undoubtedly, but the police wouldn't want news spreading prematurely. But they'd treated him like a second-rate citizen when he'd arrived early this morning. He was here to help; a little civility wasn't much to ask for. He was feeling truculent. Sod the rules.

"I should leave you alone."

"No, no, no," he stopped her, hopping up from the boot of his car, to turn and rummage through the clutter. "Bones are my speciality, you see. I can identify animal bones at twenty paces. What bone. What animal."

"Seriously?"

"Seriously. And this is a pig bone." He offered her a short, stocky bone that could have made a good club. A protrusion at one end, a smoothed ball. A wider bulbous spread at the other end. "Leg bone," he continued. "See the ball here, where it slots into the hip socket." He turned the bone over in her hands to point out the ball, fingers brushing against her hand. Jesus, Beryl thought, he's trying to chat me up over dead animal bones.

"And this is what was dug up?" She gave him the bone back.

"No, this is just my collection. For work," he quickly added. "But it wasn't a pig femur they'd found. Christ knows what kind of pigs they have running around here to think that was from a pig. The femur they found was more like this..." he leaned back into the boot. "I have a resin model."

He passed her a brown bone, sharing some characteristics with the pig bone, only that this was distinctly longer, the ball protruding more, better defined. Beryl held the femur in both hands, judging the weight, thinking to herself what animal this was from if that little stubby thing was from a pig. This had much longer legs. "A little horse?"

He laughed, not unkindly. "Come on, if you folks are all gossiping about this, you're not hoping for the burial of a little horse are you."

Her smile dropped. "This isn't...?"

He took the bone from her, held it up vertical and put it against his own particularly bony thigh. "Not a bad match."

"You're telling me there's a body out in the woods?"

He shrugged. "I'm saying nothing."

"There's a body in the woods? A person?"

Again he shrugged, as if he was starting to regret having spoken to the girl. "Make sure you pay your bill, eh?"

Beryl put her book down on the grass and hugged her knees. The book was open at a page, spine upwards, a terrible habit she was getting too old to grow out of. The heat was still oppressive, even though the worst of the afternoon was over. She was in the shadow of the campanile, the bell tower, inspired by Italian village architecture and recreated in Wales. It stood at the corner of a small green surrounded by holiday properties for rent; this section of the village closed off to day trippers and only available for residents. Her own flat not backing on to this cliff-top part of the village, Beryl wasn't completely sure whether she was allowed to be here either. But no one had challenged her, and she had been looking for somewhere to come and sit that was neither her own flat, nor anywhere near the hotel.

"This is one of my favourite places to come."

She wasn't sure if the comment was directed at her, or if she was overhearing someone else's conversation. She looked over her shoulder, to find Adrien standing close by, looking out at the view of the estuary.

"Back to the garden today? You weren't dressed for gardening yesterday," she commented. "Have you been to court?"

He laughed lightly, almost sounding like a cough. "It might well have been. I was at planning meetings most of the yesterday. Long term plans for the gardens and the village. Huw was supposed to go, but he decided to take a couple of days off and volunteered me in his stead."

"I'm sure it will have been fine. Didn't I hear you're a trained architect?"

"Yes, that's true." He looked a little uncomfortable with the subject. Surprised that she knew about that. "Anyhow, Huw's been called in today; emergency meeting with management."

"About what the police are doing in the woods?"

"Yes. I couldn't get in to take a look this morning. They had a couple of guard dogs on the woodland path. I don't know what's going on. All I've heard is Dafydd's story, which is suitably vague. It ranges from pieces of wood to animal remains depending on how he's telling it."

Beryl stood up. She could never quite work out where she was with Adrien. Some occasions, such as now, he was quite pleasant, almost charming. And other times he was impatient, as if he were wishing that she had never come to the village, and was all but saying to her to go home.

He stuffed his hands in his trouser pockets and looked back out to sea. "Did you ever see that old sixties television series they filmed here?"

"*The Prisoner*? Of course."

"Funny, isn't it? Decades ago and nothing's really changed."

Beryl glanced across at him, not sure what he was referring to.

"Adrien!"

They both turned. Huw Dodd was marching across the lawn towards them, red-faced, whether from the heat or anger it was difficult to say, but there was a definite look of determination about the way he walked.

He reached them, looked at Beryl, eyes slightly narrowed, and started speaking in Welsh. Clearly he was talking to Adrien, because Beryl couldn't follow any Welsh at this kind of speed, yet he continued to look straight at her. Was he trying to drop a hint that she ought to leave, as this was a private conversation? It hardly seemed necessary considering she couldn't understand him. But the atmosphere and the intonation were possible to read, and it wasn't pleasant. She bent down to pick up her book.

"Huw, you're being rude," Adrien interrupted him.

The Welsh faltered mid stream, Huw looking as though he'd just been slapped. Even Beryl was a little taken aback by this, her hand hovering for a moment over the book before she picked it up and straightened.

"There's three of us here, and you know we're not all fluent in Welsh."

"How bloody rude I am," Huw started up sarcastically in English. "It doesn't matter whether she understands or not. But if you want to be shown up in front of your lady friend, be my guest. I've only taken two days off and look at the mess you've left? I've even had to be called in for an emergency meeting because the police have now taken up residence in Portmeirion. You've got the police digging in the gardens. And they're not telling us yet what's going on. Not till it's fully investigated."

"We'll be told soon enough."

"You know they're digging near the little reservoir."

"I know."

"I went down there to try and find out something. Those idiots wouldn't tell me nothing. I even tried talking to some forensic fella wandering about in overalls. He wouldn't answer my questions, but had a load of questions for me about some girl he'd been talking to, pretty thing in a polka dot dress, he was telling me..."

Beryl felt her stomach crunch. She was wearing the same dress as yesterday.

"... a guest apparently, and he was having a nice long conversation with her yesterday morning about his work." He was staring steadily at Beryl. "So what did he tell you, girlie?"

"Nothing much." Beryl pursed her lips, worried she was going to start stammering. Huw was very intimidating. She ought not to let him bully her like this; she was certainly old enough to stand up for herself. But there were times when her confidence just drizzled away, and she was left with gaps, incompetent and ready to back away from the problem. She didn't want to have this conversation with Huw.

"He told you what they're doing in the woods." Huw leered up at her.

"He didn't say anything about it. Nothing definite. He just insinuated."

"Bloody hell, telling a stranger and not the people who need to know."

"Huw, give it a rest," Adrien told him. "None of this is Beryl's fault."

Huw ignored the under gardener. "So what did he tell you? So sorry, insinuate I mean. Dafydd's told me he thinks he's dug up some pig bones."

"He didn't think it was pig bones."

"Your forensic friend?"

"Huw..."

"So what did he think they've got?"

If I tell you, will you leave me alone? "He showed me a model femur. A human bone."

"Bloody hell!" Huw roared, then he was back off in Welsh, gesticulating at Adrien. He pushed at Adrien with both hands, as if trying to start a fight, which seemed like out of proportion bravado considering Adrien was the younger and taller of the two. Beryl clutched her book, not wanting to have to break up fisticuffs.

"Give it a rest, Huw." Adrien stood his ground. "You're crossing bridges before you've got to them."

Huw took a few steps back, as if conceding this wasn't going to achieve anything. He pointed a finger at Adrien. "This is your fault, Conway," he told him. "Just you remember that."

Beryl watched Huw Dodd, head gardener of Portmeirion; stalk back the way he had come. How on earth could anyone ever have fallen in love with that thing? "What was that all about?" she asked.

"Nothing," Adrien replied darkly. "Absolutely nothing."

Beryl collected the off cuts of wood in a wicker basket. Straightening, she balanced the basket on her hip and gazed out to the sea. The timing had worked well today; high tide had been in the early morning whilst most were sleeping. It gave the fisherman an excuse for a lie in, and left the day essentially undisturbed for everyone else.

"Why do you have your workshop up on the cliffs?"

Rufus (Adrien) paused in his work at the question. He was planing the edge of a new door for one of the villagers. The old door was now so swollen with salt water that it did not fit, and was far too awkward a warped shape to try and adapt the door frame to. "Practical reasons," he said. "I have freshly cut wood here that needs to dry out, and I have items I'm half way through making. Nothing would ever dry out if I kept it in the village. I can't afford to build an entire workroom and storage area watertight."

"No, I don't suppose anyone has that much watertighted," Beryl agreed. The Seagull Inn was possibly one of the most secure properties, as each guest room, as well as Arabella (Cerys)'s parlour were safe from the rising tides. Most properties only had one safe room. Yet even the Seagull Inn had its weak points. When the tides had subsided a few days ago, she had spent a good deal of time helping Arabella (Cerys) to scrape all of the seaweed out of the bar area. She'd found barnacles on the undersides of chairs, a starfish coiled up in the glass globe of an oil lamp.

"And it is very peaceful up here," Rufus (Adrien) added, putting the plane to one side. He looked over his little storage yard, fenced off, set in the woods on the cliffs. He had a neat and cosy workshop housed a wooden building to one side, which made a good shelter when the weather was unpleasant. Some days he would sleep up here instead of returning to the village to exist underwater for a few hours. Today the weather was extremely pleasant and he had brought his work outside. He looked at Beryl, who was staring thoughtfully out to sea. A light breeze whipped the loose hair back from her face. "What are you thinking?"

"I'm thinking about how ridiculous it is that the village should suffer so. I'm thinking someone should go and speak to Savant."

"Someone?"

"Me."

Rufus (Adrien) laughed, not unkindly, but amused at her naïveté, her hope in the goodness and logic of people that often didn't exist. "I don't think it would do any good, but regardless of that fact, you could hardly go now."

"Why not?"

"Well, he's a king," he faltered, searching for words that would not accidentally cause any offence. "You're perhaps not dressed for court."

"And what's wrong with the way I'm dressed?" Beryl laughed, taking his point, but stretching out her long dark skirts with a graceful hand. Moving as if almost to start a dance, and neglecting the basket of off cuts. It slipped in her hand, the brim tipping forward, pieces of wood tumbling towards the light. Beryl let out a small cry, stepping sharply back. Rufus (Adrien) caught the two pieces of wood that fell out, replacing them as he tipped the edge of the basket back up to the horizon. She was quite breathless, her arm over the top of the basket, hands clutching at the sides of the wicker. She watched the carpenter's hands move around the top of the basket, as if appreciating the weave, to then trace down the outline of her forearm, down to her fingers. He stepped up to her, tilting his head to kiss her. Beryl closed her eyes.

When she opened her eyes she was in a darkened, windowless corridor, lit by two regimented rows of flickering candles, the warm wax-yellow light softening the edges of the interior. She wore a silken, open-necked kimono of intricate designs, fabric sweeping down to the floor and dragging behind her, it was so long. Her hair was pinned up in a particularly complicated and three-dimensional style, wooden pins protruding from sections of waxed hair, strings of pearls suspended, hanging heavy, it felt as though she bore the weight of a crown upon her head. She moved slightly, and the clink of pearls, the rustle of silks ran smoothly down the length of the corridor. She lowered her eyelids, painted with gold and bronze shadows, eyes outlined in Arabic kohl, and began a careful walk down the corridor towards the double oaken doors at the end.

Every movement felt elongated, graceful and slowed as if she were wading through water. A push at the door, and the two great oaken panels swung back to reveal a great hall, and a sudden burst of daylight ripping at her retinas. Beryl closed her eyes for a moment, before gradually forcing herself to accept the daylight.

It was a daylight of sorts, silver, grey and cool. The hall was edged with a line of great arched windows, all facing the coast where beyond the cliffs the sea broiled in fury. The tide was coming in. At a distance the village could be made out, where the cliff edge broke apart and the land rolled down to the water in between. Already the lower houses were submerged by the waves.

Inside the manor it was disturbingly quiet, despite the visual evidence of a gale outside. Here in the great hall, there was only the crackle from the fire in the dominating marble fireplace. The usual furnishings adorned the hall; full length oil portraits, deep red velvet curtains, displays of swords and pistols, stuffed animal heads, and furniture of unsurpassed craftsmanship.

Towards the end of the corridor a man stood by a window. His face was turned away from Beryl, attention focused on the scene outside. He had greying hair that draped limply to his shoulders, where a fur lined cloak continued the overall sensation of resigned brooding to the wooden floor. One hand was up to the window, a breath away from touching the glass, but not quite, a thin oval of condensation formed where the point of contact may eventually happen. There was a large gold ring on one finger, a broad band with a weighty ruby set into the metal.

Beryl walked up the length of the great hall, her footsteps echoing along the panelling; the many strings of pearls clattering together. The sound resembled seashells being washed up on the shore by a gentle tide. It was perhaps this that distracted the man from the window. He shifted slightly, and looked at Beryl. She was startled to see that he looked remarkably like Huw Dodd, only with a grey beard and far longer hair.

She halted a couple of meters from him, and curtseyed. Her head lowered, knees bent, she remained in that position until he made a sound that she could rise again.

"King Savant," she stared, still looking at the floor.

"I do not know you."

"I have come from the village."

"The village?"

"By the sea."

"Ah," he looked back to the window.

Beryl's eyes widened, realising she was losing him already, his attention draw back to the waves. She got the impression this was all he did all day. "Your Majesty," she started, a little louder than was strictly necessary, making her presence more immediate than the seascape beyond the window. "I come because of the village. To beg for your help."

"My help?"

"The village suffers daily with the tides. The waters surge over the village, submerging everything. And every time, when the water has subsided, they must clean up. Everything in their lives is dictated by this excessive tide."

"There is nothing I can do."

"These tides are caused by the King Nevent. If you could give up the feud, this turmoil would cease."

He had a glazed look in his eyes as if he wasn't listening. "Give up?"

"Yes, give up."

"I have nothing more to give up."

"Call a truce on this terrible feud."

He sighed. "I don't remember anymore."

"Remember what?"

He turned back to the window, reaching up with one hand, and looked melancholic. The interview was over. Beryl felt angry; he wasn't even listening to what she was saying. And he could resolve this problem so definitely and completely, but instead he chose to live in his palace, on pause, simpering out of the window. She wanted to step up to him, turn him around and slap him. Wake him up; bring his conscience back if nothing else. If he was a king then he had responsibility to his subjects, the people whose lives he was destroying with his self-involved thoughtlessness.

That wasn't going to work. She was aware of the butler in the periphery, hovering awkwardly, eager for her to leave. She hadn't been enough of a distraction, and now it was time to leave the property.

Beryl turned away, frustrated, squeezing her eyes shut. She really shouldn't cry – the crying technique wouldn't work on a man like that, and even genuine tears were a waste of time. Her hair fell in waves across her shoulders and she slumped to the ground, skirts billowing up around her. This was all so very futile.

When she opened her eyes she was no longer in the manor, but back in the village. Somehow she had returned in time before the tides had engulfed the village. She brushed her hair behind her ear, noting that the strings of pearls and hair ornaments had gone.

"I'm glad you got back in time before the tide had risen."

She looked up from the carpeted floor. Rufus (Adrien) was stood in front of a warm, crackling fire in the hearth. They were in the watertighted room in his cottage.

"I tried, but he wouldn't listen."

"Don't blame yourself."

"I should have done something to make him take notice. Something more."

"The king's mind wanders," Rufus (Adrien) told her. "There is nothing you could have done." He dropped down to a knee in front of her. "Many have tried. But the cause is lost. We can only hope for an early end."

He meant the king's death. Beryl lowered her eyes.

"You look very beautiful this evening. Like a princess. He should have noticed you." He paused. "I notice you."

She felt something catch in the back of her throat. Expectation. Hope. Looked up at him, almost expecting him not to be there, for this to all be her imagination. Although it was of course her imagination, this was dreaming. It felt very real when Rufus (Adrien) leaned forward, kissing her on the mouth. She was a startled mouse for a moment, then returned the kiss, pulling him closer. The sensitivity of her skin increased, intensely aware of the silken weave of the kimono against her otherwise naked skin. Leaning back into the soft bedding and plump pillows on the bed, the weight of Rufus (Adrien) above her. Just don't wake up yet, she called to her other self. Don't wake up.

Beryl woke up in a particularly good mood. Following a leisurely breakfast, she decided to brave the building heat of the day and go outside. Taking yesterday's local paper and a paperback, she strolled out of the flat and down to the sea front. On the way down, near the steps up to the golden Buddha statue, she passed Adrien. He was watering bedding plants in a large carved stone tub. She gave him a silly smile, like an infatuated school girl. He stared back, confused and irritated by her, but not enough to ask what the joke was. It was only when she'd walked too far down the road to be able to gaze into his eyes, that she realised that it had been Rufus, not Adrien, she'd made love to last night. A figment of her imagination. She was grinning at Adrien about something he'd never done. Thank god she hadn't said anything. She blushed a violent red the rest of the way to the sea front.

Settling on a bench, she unfolded the newspaper she'd bought yesterday but neglected to read. A few days after the 'pig bones' discovery the police had been ready to issue a statement. It was also a hint for help from the general public. The site had been more fully excavated and the bones belonging to an adult female aged in her twenties had been removed. An adult female. A human being. There were no pig bones at the grave site. The bones had been sent to Bangor University for further analysis. Perhaps they were going to carbon date the bones, Beryl mused. Just because human bones were dug up, didn't mean that there was necessarily a murder or suspicious circumstances involved. Those bones could be hundreds of years old. It couldn't be that serious, because the police hadn't closed the village down to the general public, only requested that a short section of the forest walk was kept "temporarily unavailable".

She lay the paper down on her lap and looked along the short section of coastal promenade framing the hotel. The skinny man, the archaeologist – zoologist or whatever title he went by, was standing at the edge, hands in pockets and cigarette sticking out of his mouth at a jaunty angle. He had been quite forthcoming with information the previous time she'd bumped into him, and hadn't Huw Dodd mentioned that he'd been asking after her? "I've just been reading about your bones in the paper," she called out, holding the now rolled up paper in the air like a flag for attention or a token to denote a right to speak.

His eyebrows were raised, and for a moment he didn't move, didn't bother to see who had spoken, if the comment had even been directed at him. Then he casually glanced across, pleasantly surprised to see the girl in the polka dress from a few days past.

"My bones?"

"Yes, the pig bones that clearly aren't pig bones."

He strolled across to her, flicking the cigarette into the water. "This hasn't cut your holiday short?"

"My holiday? Why would it?"

"Oh, I don't know," he sat down on the other end of her bench. "Only the discovery of human remains might make some people a little on edge. I bet some people have left early. Of course, there's the other side of the coin, with the morbid bystanders."

Beryl felt herself blanch. She had severely misjudged their free exchange of information, albeit rather one sided. Even her own reasons for being drawn to the discovery. "Am I a morbid bystander?"

He broke out into a grin and winked at her, the rather severe tone disappearing as quickly as it had appeared. "Certainly not. Although I think you are curious."

Was that a polite way of saying mind your own business? "It was all written in the paper."

"Yeah, they had a press conference yesterday."

"So if the bones have been removed, why are you still here? Shouldn't you be analysing them back at the lab?"

"The bones are out but we're not finished. We're excavating the site a little more, in case there's anything else to be found. Archaeologists make excellent crime scene excavators, and I offered to stay and help. For a payment of course."

"So it's an archaeological site."

"It's a crime scene."

"But I wouldn't have thought you'd have known that yet, for certain I mean. All you know is how old that woman was when she died. But you don't know when she died. She could have been buried there for hundreds of years."

He grinned. "Not with that dental work she wasn't."

"Oh," Beryl faltered. A murder in Portmeirion? This idyllic fairytale-book little village. Bad things shouldn't be possible here. "How long ago do you think...?"

"Do I think she's been in there?" he finished the question. "Twenty, thirty years max. You know, they've starting calling her Number Six in the absence of her real name – the police, I mean. Which is stupid really, because Number Six was a man."

"He ran off with the butler in the end, didn't he?"

"Something like that." He looked thoughtfully across at her. "And which number have you been assigned?"

She laughed lightly. "I've not been initiated into all that."

"So what do you go by?"

"Beryl."

He laughed. "Beryl? Right. But seriously." He waited for an answer, receiving nothing more than an icy stare. "That really is your name, isn't it?"

"My mother never liked to run with the crowd."

He was mentally kicking himself. It was not exactly smooth to laugh at a woman's name.

"Jeff!"

He looked over his shoulder at the sound of his own name blared out across the village. The head of the crime scene investigation, an older man nearing fifty, was walking in their direction from the hotel. It looked as though the break was over.

"You done now?" the man asked. "We should probably get back to work."

"And that's my cue to leave," Jeff said, standing up. He faltered for a moment, as if he wanted to say something more, then changed his mind, waved goodbye and headed after his boss.

Beryl leant back against the bench and stared out across the estuary. A dead body buried in the woods at Portmeirion. At the most it had been there thirty years. She wondered who it was. It would make a fantastic story.

Noel was drunk. Not to the point where his head might drop into his soup at any moment, and he would sleep through the rest of the night – more the pity for everyone involved. He was inebriated at a level where everything he said bypassed the thought stage, and every insensitive, politically incorrect thought spewed out of his mouth like an erupting volcano. He thought it was hysterical but really it was just embarrassing.

Noel had contacted Beryl earlier in the day, suggesting dinner at the hotel restaurant, with the promise of a couple of 'writer friends' showing up – none of whom had put in an appearance yet. Anticipation tight in her chest over who she might meet that evening, Beryl had taken great pains over her appearance, pulling out a dark green 1960s cocktail dress, arranging her hair just so, and hurrying down to the hotel to promptly arrive ten minutes early. Noel was already in the restaurant, an outward curve of a room with maritime light from the sea front reflected in through the wide assembly of sash windows. Collapsed at a table set for four, Noel was already half way through a bottle of wine – most certainly not the first of the day.

He hadn't wanted to talk books or writing, refused to say which writers were coming – was rather vague on their appearance in general; and instead of usual topics of discussion, he was quite content to take the stance of a nasty tabloid paper, full of gossip and twisting the facts.

"You'll have heard about the fellow they've dug up in the woods, won't you, Beryl?" he questioned rhetorically, getting straight into the main subject for the evening.

"I think everyone knows about it. It's a bit hard to ignore."

"A bloody body," Noel swigged back the last of his wine in the glass. "Except it's not bloody is it, ha ha! Far too rotted for all that. I wonder what's been going on. This place looks so idyllic, nothing bad would ever happen here. But scratch the surface and you'll find the rot..."

"Good evening. Are you ready to order?" A waiter stepped up to their table.

"About time," Noel shook his menu. "I'm ready."

Beryl leant forward, clutching her menu, to speak to Noel as if out of earshot of the waiter. "Shouldn't we wait for the others to arrive?"

"They're not coming."

Beryl sank back into her chair.

"Oysters, I think," Noel decided. "What about you?"

"I don't know."

"Make it two," he told the waiter. "What do you make of all this police business? It wasn't you who did the deed? A customer who couldn't pay?"

Noel rolled off into laughter. The waiter was a true professional, keeping his face neutral, his tone polite. "Some of our guests tonight are of a more nervous constitution. We'd appreciate it if you could discuss the matter a little more quietly."

The laughter stopped. Noel's joviality creased up, casting shadows. "Or else? What will you do? Dig another trench next to the last one and throw me in?"

Beryl felt herself blushing on Noel's behalf. He really ought to shut up. "Noel, I think you need to drop it."

"Drop it! People need to be warned. Be protected..."

"Sir, I..."

"It's all right, Patrick." The hotel manager, the same man Beryl had seen speaking to Dafydd when the bones had first been unearthed, was at their table now. The waiter dissolved into the general background. Had they been expecting this; the manager on hand for when Noel became too much? Beryl wondered if this was a regular occurrence, and if that was the case, why on earth it was tolerated.

"I think it might be better if we move your party to a private dining area."

"So you can do away with us without any witnesses?"

Beryl snapped her menu shut. She really wasn't hungry anymore. "I think I'm going to go home."

"No!" Noel panicked as Beryl got up from the table. He staggered up, getting one of his feet tangled up with his chair legs, sending him stumbling into the hotel manager. He straightened himself and followed Beryl.

She'd come out through a door other than the one she'd entered, and found herself in an empty corridor. She'd probably get out somewhere if she kept moving; at the moment she'd quite happily hop out of a window if it meant she could get out of this hotel and back to her sanctuary.

"Beryl, wait up for me!"

She felt her heart sink, realising that Noel was indeed following. She paused, turned slightly on her heel to look back at him. What a bloody mess. And here was the great, internationally renowned author stumbling down a corridor, looking like something the cat threw up.

"This evening hasn't gone to plan."

She was feeling increasingly irritated. "Did you even invite those writers?"

"No," he admitted, a little sheepishly as he approached. "Look, this has gone a bit askew, and we don't need to sit in a room full of those toffee-nosed arseholes. Come up to my room and we'll have much more fun."

He'd pushed her up against the wall. The sudden, quite expletive intention left Beryl too shocked by the direction this evening had taken to think of a comeback or realise that she needed to get moving before this went too far. His clammy hand was on her leg, and he was leering on into her like an alcohol-fuelled vampire. "No," she said, trying to push him off, but Noel was a heavy, stubborn lump to get to do anything.

"Don't play hard to get now."

"Noel!" She shouted as she slapped him around the face. Noel leaned back from her, and there was an awful moment of silence. Beryl was shocked that she'd done it; she wasn't always the most confident of people when it came to stating her own case. Noel had been knocked over into another dimension of consciousness, his mind boggling at the after effects.

She didn't really know what else to say. "I'm leaving." She wriggled out of his grasp and marched down the corridor. She ended up in the kitchens, Kev the Liverpudlian waving at her in amused confusion, as she hurried straight through and out the back door where the sous chef was having a cigarette.

It was whilst sitting in the shade in the colonnade that it occurred to Beryl what else she had rejected last night. She opened her eyes suddenly, squinting out at the bright sunlit garden beyond the shadows of the colonnade.

She had turned down a night in Noel Farthing's bed. Of course, in many respects this had been the only course of action. He was drunk, she wasn't attracted to him, and a night with someone like that was always going to cause complications in the future. She didn't want to waste any more time with the wrong kind of men. But as her mind wandered and she thought of the what ifs, she contemplated that this hadn't just been anybody, but Noel Farthing. Author of *Fishbowl*, the author the whole world was waiting expectantly for the follow up novel. Getting involved with Noel would have given her far greater access to the book; to his entire literary career. Just imagine if it had led to something more serious. She wouldn't have needed to worry about money again. The literary groupie. Publishers would have taken her more seriously because of the connection. It would have presented new possibilities. She could have been published as well. She wouldn't have to drudge through those crumby administrative jobs. But she'd turned it all down.

Slapping her forehead, Beryl closed her eyes. All those possibilities gone. But at what price? Having Noel sweating and heaving over her, before passing out in a drunken slumber, Beryl trying to extract herself from the flabby limbs, sneaking out to the bathroom, ever so filthy, trying to wash away the shame. No, she didn't suppose she could have lived with herself.

"You feeling all right?" Cerys was walking down the length of the colonnade. "Just saw you hitting yourself in the face."

Beryl smiled weakly. Her thoughts on Noel were not something she wanted to share, no matter how nice Cerys was. "Just thinking."

"Not good for you." Cerys sat down beside her, a rolled up newspaper in her hands. "How are things? I've not see you for a couple of days."

"All right. How about you? Has work come to a halt for the police?"

Cerys grimaced. "We're allowed to work at other parts of the properties. But you're always aware of the police roaming about. We've all been interviewed."

"Really?"

She shrugged it off. "Just routine, you know. And besides, I've not been here long enough to help them that much. But work's not a lot of fun. It's tense, you know what I mean? It's like we're all under suspicion, even though we've not done anything. And we're all wary of each other, a bit short tempered. It's not good. I'm really glad it's Friday; I've got the full weekend off and I feel like I'm ready for a break from the place. A few of us are going into Porthmadog after work for a bit of an unwind. You should come with us."

"Maybe," Beryl mused.

"So you'll have heard about the body."

"Of course, everyone has."

"But the latest news."

"I'm not sure what the latest news is."

"You'll have heard that they sexed the skeleton, right?" Cerys asked, noting Beryl's nod of confirmation. "They'd sent the bones to Bangor University for carbon dating – there was some talk of them being hundreds of years old, and the police not needing to get involved. They still don't know the results, I suppose these tests take weeks, but they're reckoning the body was buried somewhere between ten and twenty years ago, give or take."

The archaeologist had been right. "How can they be so specific without the tests?"

"Dentistry apparently. Something about what was used to fill a hole in one of the teeth. No one really uses it these days, but it wasn't around thirty, twenty-five years ago."

"But that doesn't necessarily mean that the body wasn't buried a year ago. All it says is that it's been there less than thirty years."

"Yes, well," Cerys shrugged, not privy to all of the police's logic. No doubt there was more information the general public wasn't allowed to know of. "That seems to be the time period they're focusing on. They've pulled a lot of cold cases, missing people, you know. They've applied for the dental records, so they can start comparing them to the skull. It's gruesome but it might bring closure for one family." She unrolled the local paper. "They've got a list of the women they're looking into. It doesn't seem right that they've released this to the press."

"Maybe it was leaked."

"Maybe. But you should take a look." Cerys opened up the paper at the relevant page and passed it to her.

Beryl glanced over the list of names, surprised by how many there were. She probably led a sheltered life; she'd not expected more than one or two. Missing people rarely came into her scope of experience, therefore she didn't imagine it happened very often. She was probably being very naive. "It's a lot of people."

"Take a proper look," Cerys insisted, pushing the paper back at her when she tried to return it. "About half way down."

Local Welsh women's names were meaningless to her, but she pretended to study the names to humour Cerys. Then a name seemed to highlight itself. "Ffion Owen," she read out loud.

"Exactly," Cerys said, taking the paper back this time. "Apparently shortly before she walked out of this job and went travelling she had a really big bust up with her parents, moved out of their house and stopped speaking to them. Adrian said they were really angry that she'd told them she was involved with a married man. They're quite religious, see. When she left her job and Wales, they reported her missing."

"She's never bothered to contact them since?" Beryl breathed.

"No. People can have a real talent for bearing grudges long term."

"But that was fifteen years ago."

"I know. Even Adrien was shocked when I told him she'd been sending Huw these postcards from all over the world ever since. He said if she was mad enough to be still carrying a torch for Huw, then she was probably still mad enough to be keeping her parents in the dark."

Beryl suddenly felt sick. She looked across at Cerys, a nauseating sense of betrayal. Not that she'd ever asked for it to be a secret. She'd just assumed Cerys would have had the sensitivity to keep it to herself. "You've told Adrien about the postcards?"

"Well, yes, it wasn't a secret, was it?"

She was going to throw up. Adrien of all people. Mature, sensible, attractive, disapproving Adrien. "Oh god," she groaned. "Who else have you told?"

"No one," Cerys paused. "Look, you don't need to worry. I told him about the station, you know, how you found them. He doesn't think you've been breaking into Huw's house or anything."

"And what's Huw going to say when he finds out?"

"Nothing. Adrien's not going to tell him. Huw's barely speaking to anyone these days. Anyway, Adrien's worked with Huw far longer than the rest of us; he knows what Huw's temper can be like. Don't worry," She bumped shoulders with Beryl, trying to be reassuring. "Huw's not going to have a go at you about these postcards."

Beryl put her face in her hands.

"Don't worry about it, Beryl," Cerys said. "But you should probably go to the police with those postcards."

She blanched. "What?"

"Well, they'll want to remove Ffion from their enquiries, won't they? And it'll give her parents some peace, know she's all right. Where was the most recent postcard from again?"

"Tunisia, I think."

"Just pass them onto the police, and then they're out of your hair," Cerys advised. "I'd better get back to work. You'll come to the pub with us later?"

"Sure," Beryl lied. She had no intention of going to the pub. She felt betrayed by Cerys, however stupid that might be. To be fair, it wasn't a secret she'd asked Cerys to keep, and she was in the wrong in the first place for having taken the damned postcards. But to go to the pub and see Adrien, to be reminded of another failing: it didn't appeal.

She walked back to the flat, making plans to lock herself in, hide away from the world. Maybe she could just leave before the three months were up. Dump the postcards somewhere and get on a train back to York. The police wouldn't be interested in her.

Slowing on the steps up to the flat, she looked in horror at the bouquet of pink roses that had been left by her door, already wilting in the heat. There was a card in a white envelope, soon ripped open. *Behaved like a brute last night. Please forgive me. N.* Beryl's fingers tightened around the card, feeling the crisp edges bite into the creases of her palm. She kicked the flowers. "Fuck off, Noel."

Unlocking the door, she slunk into the flat, careful to lock the door behind her. She didn't want Noel strolling by unexpectedly, to 'apologise', whatever that might involve. Maybe she would go out tonight. All these men expecting her to behave one way or another, disappointed when she didn't quite meet up to their expectations. Who cared if Adrien was there? Cerys and Dafydd were good company, and she could get drunk, just forget all of these complications. She didn't want to be in the village this evening.

In the living room the bag of postcards was set upon the coffee table. The offending articles. Beryl stepped up to the bag a little apprehensively as if it might turn and wave an accusing finger at her. You deceitful, thieving spineless frigid little cow. Those postcards aren't yours. The police need these to remove Ffion Owen from their enquiries. Otherwise they'll start digging in a lot more than just the earth at the village. From silly little love notes, a woman who couldn't let go, to rather controversial items. She shouldn't leave them in the open like this. Picking up the carrier bag, she went through to the kitchen and put them in the bottom cupboard beside the kitchen bin, like they were recycling to be thrown out. They could stay there until she'd decided what to do with them.

The pub felt more crowded than it really was because the pub management had shuffled all the tables closer together to make a small dance area to one side. The main lights had been switched off, and more 'atmospheric' coloured disco lights were running. Lights from the early nineties that were slightly reminiscent of secondary school discos, and probably hadn't been PAT tested since. The television had been turned onto a music video channel, the volume scrolled right up. The noise filled in the gaps between lack of talking.

They were squeezed in around a small table, perched on stools that felt as though the padding had worn out decades ago. Beryl wasn't sure she wanted to be here anymore. She'd had thought she wanted to get drunk, but her irritation had quickly worn off upon entering Porthmadog, listening to the gardeners and understanding that other people had worse problems that she did. Cerys was hunched over, rolling up a cigarette before she'd nip out of the pub for a smoke. Dafydd was drinking the beer as if it was water; sweating profusely. Adrien lent up at the bar, taking a long time over buying a drink whilst he chatted to the bar maid.

"I can't be doing with it anymore."

Cerys glanced up from her cigarette.

"It's not my fault those bloody bones were there. The way he's carrying on, you'd think I'd dug them up on purpose."

She nodded, putting the cigarette behind her ear. "He's definitely stressed."

"Stressed?" Dafydd scoffed. "I know the man's a miserable git, it's his nature. But it's getting ridiculous. The shit we have to take. It's harassment in the workplace, you know. Whatever's been going on was going on long before we got jobs here. I don't see why we should have to be punished."

"I'll be relieved when the police have cleared up what's going on."

"It could take bloody months. I'm telling you, I'm not taking any more crap. I know Portmeirion's a prestigious place to work, but I've had enough. I'm looking for another job."

"Dafydd, don't do anything rash," Cerys advised as she stood up from the table. "Things'll calm down. It's the initial shock. Give it another week."

"It's just going to get worse," Dafydd truntered. Cerys went out for a smoke. "You must hate it," he continued, turning to Beryl. "Not a relaxing holiday. How long have you got left?"

"Just a couple of weeks." As soon as she'd named the time she felt ill. She hadn't really thought about how long she'd been living in Portmeirion, nor the fact that this was a temporary interim in real life. She'd have to go back. Two and a half months had already gone by. She had no plan, had not experienced an epiphany. She didn't know what she'd do when she went home. Home – a strange concept. The flat share felt like a memory now, not *home*. Portmeirion had begun to feel like a familiar part of life, but it was just a holiday. Perhaps she could get a job here – but no, she didn't speak Welsh anywhere near enough fluently; conversational niceties wouldn't cut it; and besides, working wasn't the same as lying around by the pool reading second hand paperback novels, getting up late in the morning and playing at writing. Maybe she should have slept with Noel, then she could have lived off him for the rest of her days, never having to worry about the drudgery of normality again.

"You'll be glad to get out of here, back to your place; York, isn't it?" Dafydd continued. "You want to get out of this shit as soon as you can. I know I do." He put down his pint. "Have you got any insider knowledge we haven't?"

"Me?"

"I know the papers got a list of missing people that'll be investigated. Maybe you've heard more? It'd be good to know it's coming to a close."

"I don't know any more than you do. Why would I?"

"You're mates with that fella that was working on the site."

"Sorry?"

"The guy on the forensics team. He's been talking to you."

He must mean the archaeologist. Beryl wished she'd never bumped into the man. Everyone seemed to resent the fact that she'd been privy to extra details through him; she who wasn't even a local. Why did she deserve to know anything more? "Have you been talking to Huw?"

"Huw?" Dafydd's face curled into a sneer. "That bastard? No way. I avoid him as much as I can. I was talking to the forensic lad, you know, scrawny, curly-haired type. English."

"Jeff."

"Is that his name? Yeah, that's the one. He was asking after you."

Adrien joined them at the table, carrying a round metal tray of drinks.

"Reinforcements!" Dafydd cried merrily, downing the remains of his current drink.

Beryl looked down at her half-full glass as a follow up was placed beside it, Adrien's long bony fingers leaving streaked prints in the condensation on the glass. She looked up at him. His hooded eyes were downcast as he distributed the drinks across what little empty space was available on the table.

"You're not still moaning, are you?" he asked Dafydd as he sat down.

"Damn right. You can't tell me you're actually enjoying coming to work at the moment."

Adrien grimaced.

"We're being punished for something we haven't done."

Adrien put his hands together, fingertips to fingertips. "It'll get better. Things will get sorted soon."

"You think Huw's going to get a personality transplant?"

"He's just got to get some things together. He'll be sorted by the end of the weekend."

Dafydd muttered something in Welsh under his breath and picked up his new pint.

Beryl sighed for no particular reason and peered down into her drink. Listened to the music. It was American pop diva evening and they were showing all the recent videos from the popular singers; girls kept skinny by the media, dressed up in barely nothing and gyrating for the teenage boys; idols for the anorexic. Urban music sung with angry faces and lots of gesticulating.

"I love this song." Cerys reappeared, still in her misshapen sweater and shapeless jeans, smelling of cigarette smoke and something slightly less legal. "We should dance." She happily grabbed Beryl's hand and dragged her away from the table to the make shift dance floor. Had either of them brought a handbag, it would have been on the floor and they'd have danced around it. Instead they danced on the spot, Cerys grinning like a crazy woman. She looked around the other dancers; a few heavily made up girls that probably weren't out of their teens yet, scrawny men that could have been anything from fifteen to thirty five, dressed in tracksuit bottoms and T-shirts; a couple of older men who had seen better days; and a handful of tourists that had somehow stumbled in here by accident.

The evening wore on, the drinks were knocked back, more rounds bought. Humours mellowed out, and even Dafydd and Adrien eventually wobbled onto the dance floor, happy drunken smiles, Dafydd's cheeks blazing red like a merry garden dwarf that had ventured out of his comfort zone for the first time and discovered the rest of the world. A number of the dancers became more and more suggestive with their moves, nudging and bumping up against bodies of the opposite sex, looking for a positive nudge back. Dafydd had taken up dancing with one of the teenage girls in a very focused way. Cerys had disappeared who knew how long ago. Time wasn't moving in a natural linear direction. Beryl felt woozy, not quite with it as if she was watching a film. Her joints were like melted chocolate, making her dancing take on a lazy, come hither tone. She shuffled to the side of the room, backing up against the wall and careful to make the slightest of moves. Now was not the time for energetic dancing. She had a bottle of something she couldn't remember the name of in one hand, a black plastic straw sticking out of the neck. It was so hot, she could feel a clammy bead of sweat running down the back of her neck and seeping into her dress. She closed her eyes, her head tilting from side to side as if her neck was made of jelly. She could have almost fallen asleep.

When she opened her eyes again, she could see that one of the older men – a forty something with a distinct belly, a striped shirt at least two sizes too small, and thinning hair, had his eye on her and was shuffling in her direction. Sober, Beryl would have removed herself from the situation before it had chance to occur. Drunk, she wasn't any more interested in drunken lecherous men, but she didn't seem to understand that she was actually present in the room for interaction, and just watched in amusement.

The video on the television screen changed and a distinctly urban, bump and grind song came on. A deep steady drum beat with an aggressive brass line that marketed where and when hips should be pushed left and right, front and back. Beryl rolled her eyes as the man started to dance particularly crudely. She thoughtlessly lifted her bottle up to suck on the straw. It would have been a screaming come on had Adrien not stepped across and broken the line of sight. Oh, it's Adrien, she thought, disapproving Adrien. They danced, somehow merging as if they'd accidentally collided in the flotsam. Beryl was moving in a fluid, slower version of the twist, her knees bending as she lowered herself, mildly surprised to see Adrien following the rhythm, coming back up in time with her. Her movements became very concentrated and slight as he moved in closer, almost pressed up against her, but not quite, a breath between them.

Someone bumped into them from the left and Beryl lost her balance for a moment, dropping her bottle. She watched it hit the floor, surprisingly not breaking, but rolling away, spilling alcohol as it went. She didn't care. I've had too much to drink, she thought as she moved to stagger off after her drink. Adrien caught her by the shoulder to stop her, and pressed her gently against the wall. The music was so loud. "I think you need to go home." He spoke in her ear.

Beryl nodded in agreement.

They got a taxi back to the village. No conversation. Beryl put her head back and closed her eyes. When she opened them again the motor was running but the vehicle was stationary. Adrien was paying the taxi driver. She made some sound to pay her share but the men ignored her. Opening the door, she stepped out onto the tarmac. The air was cooler, but she was glad this dress didn't have sleeves, because she still felt quite warm. The taxi reversed to turn around and headed back up the road. Beryl took a few steps, tottering unbalanced, and wished she hadn't worn heels. Which direction did she need to go in to get home?

"This way," Adrien said. He took her hand and spun her in an arch so she was facing the right way. Beryl headed towards the building and tripped on the first step up to her front door. She heard him sigh, then he was across and had picked her up. She was over his shoulder, gazing out down the steps as she was taken up. She was sure this was familiar from somewhere, but she couldn't think of where. An odd kind of déjà vu she'd never originally taken part in.

At the top of the steps he set her back onto her feet. "Do you have your key?" he asked, keen for her not to drop it in the dark in an attempt to find the key hole. Beryl passed him the keys. He unlocked the door and pushed it open.

"Mmmm," Beryl said, moving for the doorway in an uneven line, bumping into Adrien. He propped her up against the doorframe and glanced back into the night, uncertainty on his face as if he wasn't sure what to do. Beryl lent into the warmth of his hand. Oh Rufus, she thought, you've come back to me. Adrien stepped up against her, his mouth on hers. Tasting of beer. She kissed him back, probably not tasting any better, and stumbled into the flat, pulling him with her.

The following morning, by the time she properly woke up, he was gone. She had recollections of Adrien getting up and returning with a pint glass of water, telling her she should drink it. She'd done as she was told, then had started kissing him, and must have fallen asleep again at some point because she couldn't remember much more. Now she was awake and there was full light through the window. She suspected it was the afternoon. Stretching her limbs out full across the mattress, naked under the sheets, she stared up at the ceiling and smiled. As drunk as she had been she could remember enough of last night, and it had been better than with Rufus.

The call of nature eventually forced her from her dreamy reclining. Pulling on a dark blue silk dressing gown, she scurried through to the bathroom. Then on to the kitchen to make a cup of tea, opening the cupboard and flicking the teabag into the bin. She strolled into the living room. A cushion from the settee had been knocked to the floor, and she knelt down on it, sipping her tea and smiling to herself in the sunlight. She wondered if Adrien would come back this evening. Perhaps not tonight, he might not want to seem too eager, but she hoped he would be back soon. That it hadn't just been a drunken one night stand.

PART THREE

Beryl was a married woman. Settled in her place in life, her place in the community, her place as the wife of the village carpenter. It was barely two months since the wedding at the little church, she was still a newlywed driven by euphoria. It was morning, sunlight glinting in through the kitchen window. She stood by the table kneading bread and humming to herself, thinking through a piano lesson she would be giving that afternoon.

She paused in her baking, leaning back, hands resting on top of the dough. This was really tiring work. And not necessary; there was a bakery in the village, but she'd woken up this morning with a curious desire to bake her own bread.

A second pair of hands appeared on the dough, and she smiled as she felt her husband step up behind her. "Good morning, wife," he said, the vibrations of each word tumbling down the side of her neck. She burst out laughing as he abandoned the dough and wrapped his arms tightly around her body, pulling her away from the table. They danced around the kitchen for a moment, before he tripped and they landed together in a wooden chair by the window.

Beryl shuffled around on his lap so she could see his face. "Good morning," she replied, running fingers through his hair as she kissed him.

"It's a better morning for seeing you."

She grinned. "Just don't get too sentimental."

The smile dropped off his face. "I do mean it," he said, rather too gravely for the moment. "You know I'd never do anything to hurt you."

"Of course I know that. You don't even need to say it." She kissed him on the forehead and stood up. Returning to the table, she thumped the dough and rolled it into a long fat sausage shape. Glanced up.

Rufus (Adrien) was watching her, his expression very serious. "What's the matter? Has someone said something?"

He forced a smile. "No, it's nothing. Don't worry."

"All right," she said, not completely confident, but looking back to her bread.

Rufus settled into his chair. "Dreams are a strange thing," he commented, rather randomly, gazing off at the ceiling.

"This is like a dream," Beryl agreed, looking around the kitchen before settling her vision on him. "It's a very good dream."

"You needn't worry, this is not a dream."

She opened her mouth to contradict him, for she knew better, but stopped. There was no point trying to convince him of something he'd never be able to comprehend. Why try to spoil this beautiful escape just to prove a point?

"I had a strange dream last night," Rufus (Adrien) told her. "Very strange and so incredibly real. As if my real life had never existed. When I woke up here, well, I couldn't quite believe it for the first few minutes."

Beryl smiled. "So what was your dream about? Was I in it?"

"You most certainly were. We both lived in the village."

"It doesn't sound so different from how it is now."

"No, not this village," he corrected her. "And we didn't live together. I had a little cottage of my own, and you lived in the upstairs accommodation of another's house. I worked as a gardener, and there was so much to look after. It was too much for one man, so there were a lot of gardeners working there."

"Was I a gardener?"

"No, you didn't seem to do anything."

Beryl's kneading slowed a little.

"That was the strange thing about the village. No one really lived there, not in the proper sense of meaning. No one stayed and married, raised families; there was none of that. Most of the people in the village left at the end of the day, they were only there for a few hours. Some people stayed there on a temporary basis, people like you. These people didn't really do very much. Many of them stayed in an inn at the sea front." He paused, shaking his head in amusement. "Some fool had built a boat, but out of rocks, and built it into the sea wall. It wasn't going anywhere."

Beryl had a moment of panic. This wasn't a dream world he was describing, this was Portmeirion. Calm down. He's a projection of you. He's just telling you what you know. But she couldn't help herself; she had to state her territory, her right to exist. "That's not a dream world. That's real."

He smiled. "No."

"Really, that's real life. That's where my full life is. This here, this is just a dream."

"No, don't worry, dear heart," he contradicted her, standing and striding across to the table. "This is real life and I'm very glad for it. Because I did not like the man I had become in the village."

She stared down at the dough, beginning to feel a little sick. "Why?"

"I'd done some bad things in the past." He paused. "And I was doing something very bad to you. I was a lair, and you were just a pawn."

Her fingers squeezed suddenly into the dough, making it splurge out in all directions, gloopy ribbons flopping onto the table.

"Dearest, are you all right?"

"Quite well." She jolted away from him as if he carried a static charge. Abandoning the bread, picking strings of dough off her fingers, she hurried across the room and took down her black crocheted shawl from the hook. "I just need some air, a quick walk by the sea."

"Well let me come with you."

"No!" She almost shouted as she stepped out of the front door. "Don't let me keep you from your breakfast. I'll be back soon. Don't worry."

It was the first time she'd experienced a need to get away from Rufus (Adrien). A feeling as though the walls, the ceiling, the floor, were all moving closer together and she was about to be crushed somewhere in the middle. Pulling her shawl around her shoulders, she hurried down the street, reaching the railings at the sea wall. Gasping for air, clutching the fence, she leaned forward as if she was about to throw up. Squeezed her eyes shut. This wasn't happening. This was just a dream. Everyone here was a product of her imagination. Her life wasn't just in Rufus (Adrien)'s head, for if that was true, then how could she actually exist? This place couldn't be real, for she had no history in this world; she couldn't remember where she had come from before she arrived in this village. Had no childhood, no people, no home ground. Or what if they were all in the imagination of someone else, products to be played with in fleeting moments to pass the time? But never really existing.

The light salty breeze brushed up through her hair. She opened her eyes and looked out to sea. The tide had retreated, the beach exposed. The sand had an almost iridescent, magical glow, the glittering lapping edge of the seawaters beyond. She didn't think she'd ever been on the shore before.

Leaving the railings, she approached the shore from the stone steps built into the seawall. The sand crunched underfoot, smoothly giving way to small pockets where her feet had stepped. Beryl walked out a few meters, before surveying the length of the beach. Further to her right a group of figures were hunched over, scrabbling through the sand. A few carried baskets. She wondered what they were collecting. And all surrounded by the strange coloured sand, like mother of pearl. Then further, beyond the edge of the village, the cliffs pulled up to their full height, with what looked like netting slung across their front. Perhaps to protect from landslides.

Crouching down, she saw that the shore wasn't formed of sand, but small round pebbles. Cool and smooth like silk to the touch, she dived her fingers down into the shingle, straight and true, before curling to a scoop. Pulling forth a handful, she couldn't help but gasp as she realised this wasn't stone or sand, but a great beach of pearls. The tiny orbs tumbled from the sides of the pile, clattering back down to the lay of the shore. She looked across to the beach combers further away. In a beach filled with pure unblemished pearls, what was worth more?

A man with long, rats tails-hair and a triangular hat, glanced up as he heard an approaching body. He looked a little scruffy, perhaps one might suggest poor, from the unkempt look he had about him, the slightly raggy clothes that were layered upon him, and the three-day old stubble. He nodded to her.

"Good morning."

"Good morrow, madam," he responded, still scrabbling through the pearls, his hands dressed in fingerless gloves.

Beryl peered over his shoulder. "What are you looking for?"

He paused, sat back on his haunches. "Jet."

"Jet?"

"Found one!" One of the women suddenly straightened, holding aloft a small black piece of something. Another stopped in her back-breaking search and trotted across. She took the woman's wrist, lowering the discovery to eye level. Squinting, she shook her head. "It's coal."

"What?"

"Throw it in the basket. It'll warm a soul on a long winter's night."

The women returned to the search.

"Is jet so very valuable?"

"Oh yes, madam," the man assured her, standing up. "The ladies in the city love to adorn themselves with jewellery carved from jet. It's very popular now and makes us a good income. The coal isn't wanted, but we can burn it on our fires in winter. All of these are products of plants and animals, creatures, many long since dead."

"What about the pearls?"

"The pearls?"

She stretched out her arms.

"Oh, yes," he nodded, perhaps a little sadly, as he looked down at the sands. He'd seen this so often that it was too familiar. Now blind to the unearthly beauty. "They were valuable once; a man could make a good living diving for pearls. But not now. The market's flooded with pearls."

"Why dive when there are so many?"

"This is only recent. Relatively recent. There was a time when there wasn't a single pearl upon these shores. But now they wash up onto the shore every day with each high tide. Nevent's fury unsettles the seabed and throws up all the treasures."

"The produce of so many creatures." She didn't know that much about pearls. Did the shellfish die when it gave up its little pearl?

"There are the signs of all kinds of creatures upon this beach, even the ancient ones." He pointed across to a large dark rock protruding out from the lazy waves of pearls. "There are very ancient ones embedded in the rock. You can see them in the surface. Come and see."

It was a little odd to disturb a beachcomber on his morning work and then to be invited to explore the local geology, but just now Beryl was glad of any distraction, and followed him willingly. The rock was more a hillock in its own right, the mere peak protruding from an infinity of pearls. The man scampered up with ease of a monkey. Beryl paused at the edge, sizing up a foothold almost hip level. Gathering her skirts, she put her right foot in the grove. The man turned back and offered his hand, pulling her up and giving her the momentum to scrabble up over the uneven surface to the top.

"Look, the best one is here," he told her, splashing through a very shallow rock pool.

Beryl paused on the brink of this short rocky plain at the top. Dark rock cut up with marble white and grey shapes, skeletons and spirals, strange prehistoric forms embedded into the rock. Feint memories of a time long since past. Stepping carefully across the rock, she joined him. At their feet lay a wide and intricate spiral, the panels making up the coil formed of a marble-like substance, wisps of colour cut through. It was beautiful.

"The top of the rock here is very flat very suddenly," the man said. "My grandfather remembers when the rock was very pointed. A great storm ripped off the top of the rock and revealed this."

It was breathtaking, Beryl thought, what beauty could be hidden in the dullest of objects. She raised her eyes and gazed out to sea. The amazing glittering turquoise that swelled inland.

"Damn it."

"What?" She turned, and with her back to the ocean was surprised to discover the rock was now surrounded by seawater. The tide was coming in quickly. An abandoned basket was floating in the frothy swell. Looking back to the village she could see a couple of the women hurrying up the stone seawall, the salt water splashing at their heels. "We're not going to be able to shelter on this rock, are we?"

The man shook his head. "We had better get moving."

The journey down was not as long, Beryl surprised to see the tide lapping at her foot hold. She followed the man into the water, gasping as the morning chill bit into her skin. Her heavy skirts were immediately saturated, dragging like lead weights. The water swelled again and rushed up around her waist. Looking back toward the seawall and the village, she was surprised by how far away it was. The mass of pearls were gone from view.

"We'll have to swim."

"Not a chance," the man advised, tugging on her hand as she made to start in the direction of the village. "The current's too strong, and when the water's deeper than a body, it will pull you out to sea. You'll surely be drowned."

"But what can we do?"

He didn't answer, instead starting towards the cliff, doggedly keeping a hold of her hand. As she looked up the cliffs, and the netting to hinder landslides, she realised the thick coarse nets weren't there to stop the natural breakup of the coastline. One of the other beachcombers who had been caught unawares had started to climb the netting. The man looked back at her as they reached the foot of the cliffs. The water was higher, climbing towards her shoulders, her black shawl floating out like seaweed. "Climb!" he shouted.

Finding a rung underwater to begin the ascent, Beryl really felt the tug of the current, trying to draw her out to sea. The sound was tremendous, and quite frightening. She wasn't a particularly strong swimmer and certainly couldn't fight against this. Certainly not in such heavy, soaking clothes. Her heart pumping, she began to climb, the water keeping up with her so that she never completely escaped the reach of the sea. Focus on the next rung. You'll get to the top and be safe. Roll over the edge and on to those grassy plains near Savant's palace. You'll be safe. The muscles in her arms burned in pain. She could barely force the air down her throat fast enough. Aware that the man was getting higher than she was. The woman above them seemed to have stopped. Perhaps she had run out of momentum, would soon collapse in exhaustion and plummet into the broiling depths of the sea.

They reached the top of the nets. There were still a few metres left to go before the top of the cliffs. It wouldn't be possible to climb all the way and flee to the lush grass of the cliff tops. Don't look down, an inner voice advised silently, but she couldn't help herself, and was already twisting, sneaking a look as the spray splashed her back. The water was already up to her shins. Out of the water the wind had picked up and chilled the salt water that had soaked through the fabric and lay cooling on her skin. We'll be drowned, she thought, panicking. Twisting to look at the man, "What now?" she screamed at him, her voice barely a whisper above the din of the crashing waves.

"Hang on!" He yelled back.

"How do we get to the top?"

"We don't. Stay here until the tide goes down. It doesn't usually get too much higher. Your head'll be above water."

Doesn't usually get much higher, Beryl thought? They were just supposed to hang on to the net like barnacles for the next few hours?

"Get one of these," the man advised. He was gesturing to the rope loops that hung down from the deep metal rods holding the net to the cliff face. Like oversized hangman's nooses, they dangled limply. He slipped one arm, then the next through the loop, letting the loop slip down to rest against his back; an extra support pinning him to the cliff should his arms give away or the pull of the sea prove to be too much for the strength in his body.

Beryl screamed as a particularly large wave lashed out at them, drenching her in water and throwing her hair over her eyes. The water was half way up their backs. She could feel the pull of the currents, the weight of the sea, dragging her skirts down, but worse than that was the feeling of the sea encircling her waist and trying to pull her away from the cliffs. She blindly reached up with one hand, trying to locate a loop for her own support. Like an eager lover, the sea entwined itself more securely around her waist and pulled. She felt herself drawn away from the nets, barely hanging on by three points – two feet, one hand. Oh no, she cried to herself, I can't drown now, not yet. I'm barely married. I don't want to die. The sea tugged more determinedly. Come away with me. She opened her mouth to scream as it finally succeeded and she lost her grip. Salt water poured in through her open lips and she was submerged, pulled away into the depths of the ocean, golden light and turquoise water currents drawn out like an artist's palette as the sea broiled. And she was gone.

The first thing was the intense void of sound. A stillness beyond even the drawing of a breath, of the existence of air. As if eardrums were burst and lungs were shut off, basic functions closed down permanently. Yet she could hear and she could breathe. She knew this for she could sense her lips part as she drew breath again. And now that she listened, she could hear the strange, eerie steady drip, a slow beat of water droplets that were in no rush for they had the luxury of an eternity to fall.

Beryl opened her eyes. It was a strange light, almost like the approach of dusk, an orange-silver filter. She could see her hand in front of her. A few tangled strands of hair fell across her face, cutting her vision into rectangular blocks. Something hard pressed into her right cheek. In fact, a many great solid objects were pressing in to her, little domes along the length of her body. She was lying crumpled on her side on a spread of cool damp cobblestones.

Something wet slapped into the right hand side of her nose. Beryl sat up abruptly, wiping her face. She gazed around. She appeared to be sitting in the middle of a small cobbled market place. The buildings edging it were indistinct and far away, as if this marketplace took up the entire northern hemisphere of a globe. In the very centre of the square there was a fountain in a rounded stone basin. The water spurt from the top made no sound as it fell into the pool at the bottom, in fact the general flow of the water seemed much slower, she might have thought it frozen ice but for the barely perceptible signs of movement.

"Hello?" Her voice echoed in one direction then the other. She was the only being in the square. Beryl stood up, distinctly ill at ease. Where the hell was she? As she pulled up to her full height, she shivered, realising she was wearing her drenched dress, her hair hanging like rats tails. A droplet of water gathered at the end of a coil of hair, and fell. Yet it didn't splash onto the cobbles, instead it rather slowly revolved upwards. Beryl watched it in a mixture of horror and amazement.

"Where am I?"

There was a sound. She turned, not finding the source, but hearing the sound again. Footsteps. There was someone else here. "Hello?" Running across to the fountain, she hopped up onto the rim of the pool basin to try and get a better view.

A figure was steadily yet awkwardly walking towards the fountain, growing in height and stature because of the natural curvature of the land. A tall figure, at least six foot, lumbering towards Beryl. Wearing a limp, elongated tutu, a trail of long feathers hanging from a back section; layers of draping bodices and shawls, bejewelled pins set in a nest of curled hair. A glittering locket at the base of the neck. Beryl couldn't take her eyes away from the mutilated legs. The feet and ankles looked as though they had at one time been broken and smashed in multiple places, rolled out like dough to take a new form, then left to heal in a fresh style. Feet like great wide pads, flexible to roll over the undulations of the cobble stones. Ankles that were great and long, looking double-jointed. They seemed to throb on each step, as if hydraulically powered; some strange kind of shock absorber. It gave an odd bodily bounce to each step. At the edge of the fountain, the woman-creature, now towering over Beryl, leant gracefully forward to peer at the newcomer, with great moist eyes that were two, perhaps even three times the size of what would have been expected for a human face.

Beryl could feel her breath balled up in the back of her throat. She was so taken aback by this appearance, she couldn't remember if she needed to breathe in or out just now. Although it was an intimidating figure that stood before her, hulking and yet with the nuance of being as light as feathers, she felt no malice and no threat.

"Where am I?"

The woman raised her eyebrows slightly.

"Is this the kingdom of Nevent?"

The woman looked up to the sky. She shook her head.

Beryl looked up above them. It was strange, but there was nothing there to see, not even a void. But what did this mean?

"You are somewhere." The voice was quite light and sweet, with a neat, trained elocution.

"Somewhere?"

"Somewhere forgotten."

"And you are?"

"Someone."

Someone. Beryl was beginning to sense that without the right questions, this conversation was going nowhere.

The women took a step back, her whole body nodding like a turtle dove. Beryl's eyes were again drawn back to her mutilated legs. "What happened to your ankles?" She blushed as the words left her mouth, regretful that she'd been so blunt, so curious in something that was not her concern.

"They did not want me to go." The woman turned, slowly walking away, talking dainty steps across the cobbles.

Beryl followed. "But who are they? Why am I here?"

"They?" the woman paused, caught up in the thought of parties unnamed. She twisted to look directly at Beryl. "You won't be here long. You need to go home."

"Well, that's fine," she agreed, wondering if Rufus (Adrien) would be worried about her. He would have noticed that she hadn't made it back to the cottage when the tide had risen. Maybe he thought she'd taken shelter in the church or the inn with Arabella (Cerys). "How do I get home?"

"You'll go in time."

She slowed down, feeling increasingly disorientated. The ground was sloping quite steeply the further away from the centre she walked. Ahead it looked as though it fell into a vertical drop. She looked back at the woman. "Are you her?"

"Her?" The woman slowed, her buckled legs trembling awkwardly as she turned on the spot to look at Beryl. "You want to know who I am?"

Beryl gazed at the big eyes. The ragged dress that had once been a dream. "You're the woman they're fighting over," she realised. The nameless woman that no one could quite remember; no one was really concerned about. The villagers worried about their homes, battered by Nevent's fury and Savant's stubbornness. The two kings concerned themselves on their feud, on not giving way to the other. The woman who had never asked for any of this was somehow sidelined. Quite insignificant.

"What is your name?"

"My name?" She smiled gently, touched that she was being asked this question. Her long lashes battered, as if embarrassed by the attention. "Consider me a foxglove."

Beryl stood on one of the woodland paths around Portmeirion, staring at a patch of foxgloves. She was not feeling well. She'd been a little off centre all day, but standing in the wood, looking at these flowers, was making her feel terrible. She turned away and headed back for the village.

It had been two days since she had last seen Adrien. No call, no email, no visit, not even a glimpse from a distance as he worked. Beryl didn't like to think she was the clinging, demanding kind, but this forced apathy, playing the game of hard-to-get, was wearing a little thin, especially considering they'd now slept together. She supposed it was against the rule book, but she was just going to have to go and visit him.

Scouting around the edge of the village, she headed up the hill, away from the ticket office, the car park and the afternoon's tourists, towards the little cottage she knew Adrien lived in. She wasn't surprised to find he wasn't there – he was probably at work, but she picked her away cautiously around the building's perimeter, peering in through each window. Paranoid that he might be trying to avoid her. She even tried the door. It was locked.

This was ridiculous. But she couldn't shake that anxiety. Mixed up from silly dreams of drowning and messages that Adrien had used her. Probably nothing more than an interpretation of her own insecurity that she wasn't being taken seriously, that she'd just been used for a drunken one night stand.

Waving her pass at the ticket office, she re-entered the village. Walking past the first buildings: a painted flat statue of a mermaid through an archway; the golden bird atop a rooftop. Down an ally road towards a pink building with an arched tunnel allowing passage. She paused in the tunnel, looking up at the dramatic painting on the ceiling of the tunnel. There was such incredible attention to detail in this place. Nothing was left to chance. Everything had been put there for a reason, for a great deal of effect. Every surface was decorated. There to evoke a response and an emotion from those who viewed it.

In the left hand wall of the tunnel there was a circular window above a small open archway. She stepped through, following a cobbled path towards the grotto on top of the cliffs. And like all lost things that never turned up until one stopped looking for them, Beryl found Adrien working on the rose bushes near the grotto.

"Adrien!"

He glanced up idly, noticing it was Beryl, then panicking for a moment, stumbling back, secateurs held aloft as if in signal of surrender.

"Are you all right?"

"Yes, I..." he started distractedly, looking at his surroundings as if trying to gauge an escape route, as if Beryl would chase him and try to pin him down.

"Look, I don't want to disturb you at work, it's just that I haven't..." she faltered. He didn't look as though he was listening to her. In fact, he appeared to be concentrating on a background noise, a vehicle engine. It sounded as though something was driving up the little road from the village. Adrien threw his secateurs into the nearby wheelbarrow.

"If this is a bad time..."

He snatched her hand from the air and pulled her down the path as he hurried deeper into the garden, following the curvature of the path around the side of the dumpy tower-like building at the cliff edge. Ducking in through the open doorway, he pulled Beryl into the grotto.

Beryl dumbly followed, her movements rather ungraceful as she was dragged into the grotto, the cobble stones digging into the thin soles of her sandals. The grotto, as it was named in the guidebook and architectural plans, was an open-air curved corridor on one half of the squat tower, large seashells pressed into the interior concrete-plastered walls. There was a small water fountain on the central wall that wasn't working, two elongated fish, their tails twisted around one another, heads facing three scallop shaped basins. The exterior wall was a series of openings, commanding fine views of the sea, and the direction down the cliffs to the hotel and the seawall-boat at the front.

"I just wanted to ask you about the other night," she started, feeling a little foolish. Why on earth would she think someone as sophisticated and sensible as Adrien had taken her as anything more than a little light entertainment?

He looked at her, a touch of regret, but didn't say anything. Instead he took her, pushing her into one of the openings, her shoulder blades pressed up against the blue metal bars stopping visitors falling out and down the cliffs. A hungry man, he kissed her full on the mouth, ceasing any further questions. And then he was gone, stalking back out of the grotto. Beryl slumped down onto the windowsill. More confused than before.

When she re-emerged from the grotto, still a little breathless, she saw a little buggy with trailer parked up on the road. Huw Dodd was stood by the side of the vehicle, hands on hips, speaking rather sternly to Adrien in Welsh. Beryl wished she'd been learning the language for a few years rather than a couple of months - she   might have had some chance of understanding. It probably wasn't any more interesting than which bedding plants they were going to get ready next, but there was a tension in the atmosphere that made her turn and take the winding garden path down the cliffs to the sea front, rather than walking back up to the road. She didn't want Huw Dodd to see her.

The path went through a series of whitewashed structures like toy villas, and little archways, a walled set of steps twisting and turning in their descent to the sea. At the bottom, she walked along the lower level of the wall, then up to the front of the hotel. She was still feeling distracted, paranoid without knowing what she ought to fear. Just a sensation that she needed to hurry home.

Head down, eyes to the road, she marched back up through the village, slipping past the 'residents only' sign by a side footpath, and around to the steps up to her flat. Fumbling with her key, she unlocked the door and stumbled into her temporary home, relived to be away from people. Putting the key on a side table, Beryl held up her hands, surprised to see her fingers were shaking. Why was she so nervous?

She went through into the kitchen and turned on the kettle. It was hot, but perhaps a cup of tea would calm her down. In the void of not knowing what else to do, it seemed like a good fix. She took a teabag from the opened box on the worktop and dropped it into a clean mug. When the kettle clicked off at boiling point, she poured the steaming water into the mug. Twirled the teabag around with a teaspoon, before scooping it out. Opening the cupboard under the sink, dropping the teabag into the bin, closing the cupboard door. Putting the teaspoon by the sink, picking up the mug and walking to the door.

Beryl stopped, turned and put the mug back on the worktop. She realised what had been unsettling her. What she had seen, or rather not seen. Opening the cupboard under the sink, she crouched and looked in. The bin was there, but that was all. The bag of postcards, which she hadn't given a conscious thought to for the last two days, was not there. And in all honesty, she couldn't remember seeing them since she'd first put them in the cupboard. Two days ago, early evening, just before she'd gone into Porthmadog to the pub with the gardeners. She hadn't seen the postcards since.

The atmosphere in Portmeirion never became as bad as it could have grown in other places, but it was enough to get Beryl thinking about going further afield. She would soon have been living in North Wales for three months and she had hardly seen a thing beyond the village and Porthmadog. Barely done anything constructive other than lazing around reading cheap paperback books and writing her silly short stories. Trying to learn Welsh with little success. She was stagnating.

Considering human remains had been unearthed on the village property, the hysteria about the mystery had been kept to a minimum. In other, less regulated places, the media would have descended, would have spoken and photographed everyone they could get hold of. A few journalists and a television crew had been into the village, but it had all been strictly controlled, and anyone who tried to be a little too invasive, was politely but firmly escorted from the site by village security. In that respect, the police were probably very lucky that the body had been buried on private property.

But the change was perceptible. Even the weather came out in sympathy and clouds pulled together to blot out the sun. Light drizzle fell, and when it wasn't raining, there was a melancholic dampness about the place that simply wouldn't dry out. Despite the rain, Beryl had decided she was getting out of the village for the day. She'd pulled on her waterproof jacket and walked up out of the village, along the roads past the car parks for the tourists, along the one way system that led up to the Castle Hotel where she had first checked in, and further yet, to a small village of the true meaning of a village, where the two train stations were positioned – one for the public network and one for the narrow gauge line that ran up into the Snowdonia National Park. She went under the bridge and to the mainline station at Minffordd, catching the next train heading south.

She didn't stay on the train particularly long, and got off only a few stops later at the coastal town of Harlech. A flat stretch of sands followed by dunes followed by houses and a railway line, before the gradient of the land suddenly lurched up dramatically, nestling the rest of the little town on its rocky outcrops, the imposing shape of Harlech castle looking down on the sea. She bought a ticket for the castle and wandered around the site. Inside it was mostly ruined, only the exterior shell in a good enough condition to show what it had once been. She climbed up to the rampart walls that followed the exterior of the castle; low-lying walls on either side of the high pathway making it feel particularly exposed and making her knees feel weak.

This was the end. The rain started to fall more heavily, darkening the shades of grey on the stonework, intensifying the green of the little ferns and creeping plants that somehow managed to find a roothold in the cement of the castle walls. Beryl pulled her hood up and retreated to a corner where the remains of one of the turrets stood. With her back to the wall, she crouched down and felt her eyes well up with saltwater. She had less than a week left before she would have to check out of Portmeirion. She'd been here so long, her life in York felt like a previous chapter in a book she'd once read and finished. And now the Welsh chapter would be over.

In a lot of respects it was already over. This wonderful place she had come to, the expectations, had all disintegrated. The gardeners were not the same happy bunch she had met that first morning. Weighed down by the unknown back story of that body in the woods, no one really wanted to be in the village anymore. Her writing had faltered, and the supposed inspiration from socialising with a world-renowned author had soured when he had made a drunken pass at her. She'd only seen Noel once since that awful evening, but there had been other people around, and she had neatly managed having to speak to him too much. And then of course there was Adrien, upon whom she still harboured a great many far-fetched hopes, even though she knew deep down it wasn't going anywhere. But it had all been a change to her stilted routine; something happening, something that made her feel like there could be a little more going on in life than a rundown shared flat with someone she didn't particularly like, and a mind-numbing office job run by petty-minded power junkies and bitchy colleagues who had such empty, pointless lives, there was little else to live for other than making everyone around them as miserable as they were.

She left the castle and wandered down the central street through the little town, walking through the middle of puddles, apathetic to her wet shoes. She walked past little antique shops, tourist kiosks, a small church and terrace buildings. She went into a grocery shop on a tight corner in the road and bought a newspaper and a few things for lunch. She saw that there was another article about the Portmeirion body, but it was raining so heavily outside that she didn't dare take the paper out of her rucksack to read.

Sitting under the awning of the station house waiting for the train, she listened to the tannoy announcement, first in Welsh, then English, about the approaching train. It wasn't until she was on the train, retreating to the far end of the carriage away from the noisy extended Liverpudlian family that were onboard, that she took the paper out of her rucksack and read the latest story about the Portmeirion body investigation.

Beryl put the paper down on the table and looked out of the window at the raindrops chasing each other over the glass as the train steadily clunked its way up the coast. The papers were claiming that the body had now been identified as that of Ffion Owen, a previous employee of the Portmeirion estate who had disappeared from her job and her home some fifteen years ago. But this was impossible, because Beryl knew that the woman had since been travelling the world. Up until three days ago she had even had the evidence to prove it. Surely there had to be some mistake. Perhaps Ffion had similar fillings to another woman who had gone missing – the dentist had misidentified the teeth. And because the police were so keen to get the body identified, they had leapt upon the first plausible suggestion. She wondered for a moment if Jeff the archaeologist would be back at the village anytime soon – she could perhaps try to get some more inside information from him. But no, she told herself, putting the paper back in her rucksack as the guard announced they would shortly be stopping at Minffordd. It really wasn't any of her business, and besides which, with the body removed and the area searched, Jeff's business in Portmeirion would be complete.

Beryl saw Cerys waiting in the turquoise painted shelter on the single platform on the mainline Minffordd station. Cerys was hunched up into her jacket, a cigarette hanging out of the corner of her mouth; a grubby, tightly packed rucksack set on the ground between her feet.

"Cerys!"

The woman glanced up, smiled weakly when she saw Beryl, but didn't say anything or make any movement. She watched the train pull out of the station – she was waiting for the train heading in the other direction.

"Are you going somewhere?"

Cerys took a deep drag on her cigarette and blew out the smoke slowly into the drizzle beyond her shelter. "I've just taken a few days leave. I'm going down the coast to stay with one of my aunts. I just need to get away from this place for a little while."

"How long are you going to be gone? I might not see you again before I leave."

"You leaving soon?" Cerys raised her eyebrows, surprised by this news. She knew that Beryl's stay here was only temporary; a few months or whatever Beryl had said it was going to be. But Cerys had quickly lost track of time and Beryl had become part of the scenery, something that was always in the village. "Probably for the best," she mused. "It's not the place it was. Which day are you heading off?"

"Saturday."

"Oh, I'll be back by then. I'll pop by to say cheerio." She dropped the remains of her cigarette to the ground and stubbed it out under her shoe. "Did you pass those postcards on to the police?"

The postcards. Beryl felt uncomfortable by the thought of them. "No. I don't have them anymore."

"You pass them on to Huw?"

She shook her head. "I put them in a cupboard. They've just... disappeared."

Cerys pursed her lips. "You mean they've been taken?"

"I assume so. I only realised yesterday that they're not there anymore."

"*Cach*," Cerys cursed quietly. "Huw'll be needing those postcards now, you know. Have you seen the papers today? They're saying it's Ffion they've dug up in the woods. Ffion Owen? But it can't be her because she's been backpacking round the world; sending Huw all these messages. I wish she'd left some kind of forwarding address on those postcards." She paused, glancing over at Beryl. "You know they say that Ffion was mad about Huw, but he wasn't having any of it. You know what people are like for putting two and two together and getting six."

Beryl nodded glumly.

"Ffion," Cerys said quietly to herself, staring out over the railway tracks to the sheds on the other side. "It means foxglove, you know."

Beryl shook her head. "I didn't know that."

There was a crackle through the air, static breaking through the dull atmosphere, then a voice started to impart information in Welsh. Beryl stepped back into the recesses of the shelter, suddenly feeling a little overwhelmed. Things were starting to break, to open apart. The train slowed and halted with a hiss and a judder at the platform. Cerys said she'd see her in a couple of days and climbed into the carriage. It was as Beryl was waving goodbye, that she finally realised that the postcards really didn't matter at all, and if the police were going to start throwing around theories of murder; of the body in the forest being that of Ffion Owen, the postcards wouldn't help anyone in the slightest. Because they were fakes. Every last one of them.

He wasn't answering the door but he was definitely in the building. Beryl knew that for a fact because she was looking at him through the window. She probably looked like a peeping tom, or a scrawny stalker, creeping through the back garden in the drizzle, a shapeless figure in a zipped-up waterproof coat, hood shadowing her face. Standing in a flowerbed, looking in through a window. Inside the living room Adrien sat alone on the settee, hunched forward, a glass of something that was probably a spirit, in one hand. He was staring at the carpet with a fixed look of concentration, lost to his thoughts. Beryl rapped on the window and he started, almost dropping the glass. He looked up at the window; his usually sleepy eyes wide open like a startled creature. He put the glass on the coffee table and walked to the window, squinting now and trying to gauge who was outside. Beryl leaned deeper into her coat on purpose, feeling the shadows filter across her face more perfectly.

Adrien opened one of the French doors at the end of the living room, tentatively peering out into the rainy, murky garden. "Beryl?" he said with some surprise when she turned slightly and he could see her face. "What are you doing here?"

What was she doing here? Surely they were supposed to be love's young dream. "Can I come in?"

Adrien paused, as if he didn't really want to see her, but was too polite not to let her in from the rain. "Sure," he said, not sounding particularly enthusiastic. He left the door ajar, heading back for the settee.

Beryl slipped into the cottage, pushing the hood back. She set her rucksack on the floor by the doors, then unzipped her jacket. It would be nice to get out of these rain-sodden things, but the waterproof coat would have to be the extent of her undressing this time. She noted her damp jeans, accepting they'd have to wait until she got back to the flat. She shivered; it wasn't particularly warm in this little stone cottage.

He'd taken up his drink again. There was a bottle of opened whisky on the coffee table. "Do you want one?"

She shook her head. Watched him take another drink. "It was you, wasn't it?"

"What was me?"

"The postcards that were in my kitchen cupboard."

Adrien smiled wryly, looking into his glass as if she were swimming in the whisky. "Have you come over here to accuse me of stealing?" he asked. "Because I can't really steal what wasn't yours in the first place."

"They weren't yours either," Beryl retorted. "Anyway, possession is nine tenths of the law."

He leaned back into the settee, expansively. Never offering her a seat. He seemed slightly drunk. "Yes. Cerys told me how you said you'd found those postcards. Dumped at Shrewsbury station. We have no idea how they got there."

"Did Huw put you up to stealing them?"

"Those postcards were never yours."

"It must be a bit of a disappointment to find they're not the originals."

"Excuse me?"

"Well, those are fake postcards aren't they? There's no way Ffion ever wrote them. So I guess they're not much use to Huw. Has he managed to find the originals?"

Adrien laughed at her. "You really are dim."

His arrogance knocked her off balance. Irritation balled up, wanting to hit him. He ought not to be taking the moral or intellectual high ground with her. He had betrayed a trust and stolen something from her flat. "But they must be fakes."

"And why must they be fakes, Miss Little-Girl-Detective?"

"Because they're written in English," Beryl said, her voice sounding more uncertain. She'd been so sure of her conclusions on the walk down from the train station to Adrien's cottage. That the postcards were fakes, copies, translations of the originals Ffion had sent to Huw. Huw had lost all of his postcards, perhaps he'd just thrown them out in a tantrum. Now that the police were suggesting Ffion had been buried in the woods over a decade ago, he found he was in need of his keepsakes again. Adrien had told him that Beryl had picked up the postcards, by some miraculous way in a train station in England. Huw had somehow persuaded Adrien to steal them. Unfortunately for Huw, these postcards were fakes, and would be of no use to him. "Because postcards between two native Welsh speakers would be in Welsh."

Adrien nodded in agreement. "That's all fine except for your assumption that there is another set of postcards."

"They're the only postcards? But why would Ffion write to Huw in English?"

"She wouldn't." He glanced up at her. "Ffion didn't write those postcards."

"But who would?" Beryl breathed, sitting down on a wooden stool by the door. It made no sense. Those postcards had been sent over a fifteen year period. A continuous story of one muddled woman's journey across the globe. Trying to mend a broken heart.

"That is the one question we have no answer to." Adrien downed his drink.

"So she was never travelling the world," Beryl said, more to herself than for Adrien's benefit. She looked over at him. "And no one has any idea where she really is?"

He laughed out loud at her. "We all know where she is. Don't you read the papers?"

"The papers say she's buried in the woods," Beryl stated as if this was complete nonsense. She stopped, leaning forward. "You mean she really is buried in the woods? Oh my god. Huw killed Ffion and buried her in the woods? And he's been sending himself postcards to cover his tracks..."

"For crying out loud, Beryl," Adrien snapped. "I just said no one knows about the postcards. And no one murdered Ffion. She killed herself."

"What, and she dug her own grave afterwards?"

Adrien looked sour. "No. Huw and I did that."

"Her family don't know what happened to her. They think she ran away. If it was suicide why didn't you just call the police?"

"Because things are never that simple. No doubt those gossips will have told you about Ffion and Huw, even though they weren't there at the time."

"But you were."

"Huw was still married at the time, but the divorce was kind of inevitable by then. Not that Ffion had anything to do with that. She was just a bit... a bit naive I suppose you could say. You remind me of her." He paused, looking across at her. "Not to look at, you're very different. But you're both quite naive, seeing the goodness in everything. Lacking in confidence, the gumption to do something..."

Beryl opened her mouth to protest, but couldn't think of anything to say.

"Ffion was mad about Huw. Christ knows why, because he wasn't always pleasant to her. But she was the kind of woman who over analysed everything; saw declarations of everlasting love in the everyday gestures that meant nothing. She was a lovesick puppy, the way she simpered around him. Would do anything he asked. It was really pathetic. From what I understand, she didn't come from the happiest of homes, and was looking for something better where she could get it. I suppose she saw Huw as her knight in shining armour. Of all the people she could have become infatuated with, she picked him.

"It all came to a head and Huw let her know in no uncertain terms that he wasn't interested. Huw's not what you'd call tactful, you know. There was an audience when he did it; he really humiliated her. I know I thought Ffion was weak, but she didn't deserve that..." he stopped, looking off into the middle distance, something Beryl couldn't see.

"She ran off, and we didn't see her again until late that night. Dead. In Huw's cottage."

"He broke her heart and she killed herself?"

"I told you she was weak. Thing is, she'd cut herself; bleed to death all over the living room. Huw panicked, he didn't think the police would believe him if he said he'd just found her like that in his house. She'd gotten herself a key somehow, let herself in whilst he was out at the pub. Maybe if he'd been sober he wouldn't have come up with that half-arsed scheme. I was lodging at the cottage; it was a summer job for me before I went to university. I stupidly agreed to help him bury her in the woods. We burned the living room carpet a couple of days later. Cleaned out that room. Although there's probably still traces of blood on the floorboards.

"The longer it went, the harder it was to go to the police. How do you explain that a woman broke into your home, killed herself, and then you buried her in the woods, burned your carpet and scrubbed out your house? Hardly sounds like the actions of an innocent man. A few weeks after that the postcards started. I didn't find out about them till maybe six months ago. Huw showed me them. He had a bag full of the damn things – he's been torturing himself all these years with those stupid postcards. He told me he was going to get rid of them once and for all. Try to move on. And then Cerys casually mentioned to me one day that you'd somehow found these postcards. Of course when Dafydd started digging in the wrong place and found her, Huw panicked. He wanted the postcards back, thought he could hand them into the police, throw them off the scent." Adrien leant forward, pouring another measure of whisky. He sank back into the settee.

That was the end of the story. Beryl looked down at her shoes. She thought of foxgloves. A naive, weak woman, according to Adrien, who fell in love with the wrong man. It was perfectly plausible that she would have written all those postcards. She looked over at Adrien. "The other night," she started, not sure if she wanted to ask this question. "Did you just spend the night so you could get those postcards?"

His eyes narrowed. Looked at her as if he'd just realised it was actually her for the first time. "Where the hell do you get off? Those weren't your property. All of this has nothing to do with you. Don't you realise that I'm complicit this mess? And you, pinching someone's lost property in a station, and sitting in your expensive holiday flat for three months reading someone else's personal postcards for entertainment. Were they good fun? Did you have a few laughs?"

"I wasn't..."

"None of this is any of your business," Adrien roared, leaping up from the settee. "You're just a pathetic little voyeur. Your own life is so shallow you think you have the right to poke about in other people's business. A little bit of inspiration for those silly stories you send to that idiot Farthing. You seem to forget these are real people's lives you're toying with here. There are consequences for everything you do."

"I didn't..."

"Get out of my fucking house, you pathetic little bitch!"

Beryl stumbled for the door, grabbing her jacket and rucksack on the way. She fled from the cottage, her coat flapping like a long flag after her as she splashed through the puddles, the rain battering down. Her tiny figure ran along the road towards the village, with only one thought in mind. Let me go home.

Self-pity was pathetic and served no practical use. Beryl was well aware of this fact, but just now she didn't care. Besides, it was easy to adhere to such ideals when your life wasn't scraping the dregs in the bottom of the barrel. It was three o'clock in the morning, she was slightly drunk, and this seemed like the best course of action. If she couldn't indulge herself now, when could she?

Slouching in disarray on the living room floor, she was taking a break from sobbing. Staring at the opposite wall. Her own stupidity never ceased to amaze her. She should have realised that there had been an ulterior motive for Adrien sleeping with her – he was hardly going to want to start a relationship with such a bland, gossip-driven girl like her. Shy and awkward, there was probably a good reason why her genetic makeup had aligned itself so. Keep out of the good people's way.

He had been right. This story of Ffion and Huw wasn't any of her business. It wasn't even a story, it was real life. It wasn't something to dissect and pick through for a morning's entertainment as if it were nothing more than one of Noel's literary creations. They existed, or rather in Ffion's case had existed. The situation, the unfulfilled emotions between the two lived on, even though one side had expired and the other was desperate to escape, although clearly bound here by the past. Every action had its consequence. Beryl shouldn't have become involved. She had no right. Oh, but she'd felt so self-important, so popular being accepted into the gardener's clique. As if she'd found her place, was wanted somewhere. Just another tourist, just another number. They'd probably gossiped about her as much as she'd pondered over Huw and Ffion's relationship.

Her eyes narrowed. Not that Adrien could take the moral high ground. He'd used her just to get at those stupid postcards. Postcards that were fakes. And she'd been stupid enough to skip along with the seduction, deluded in thinking it could be genuine. Her fingers tightened around her empty glass. Stupid, stupid little girl. Probably what Huw had told Ffion. You stupid girl. With your stupid infatuation.

The glass shattered as it hit the far wall, flung in anger. Shards rebounded outwards, spinning on the floor. The artificial light picked up on the cut edges of slivers. The outburst hadn't solved anything. Beryl held a sob back in her throat and looked miserably over at the side board. What a disastrous birthday present this had turned out to be. Three months of such potential, and this is what she had managed to achieve.

She toppled over onto her side, resting her head on one of the settee cushions that had made its way onto the floor. Closed her eyes. There didn't seem to be anything good left in the world.

She was woken by a gentle steady rocking. Beryl, feeling as though she had a heavy hangover, gingerly opened her eyes to semi-darkness. She felt nauseous. Moaning quietly, she leaned across, finding a catch and pulling back a thin ragged curtain. Dismal grey light greeted her, a landscape of washed out moorland, no human habitation in sight. She was riding in a carriage, perhaps a post carriage, the gentle rocking as the vehicle was pulled over the rutted earth by a team of six horses. "Where am I?" she mumbled to herself.

"You are in a horse carriage heading for the city. We'll be there in another three hours."

She hadn't realised there was another passenger in the carriage. She ought to have guessed, because this was a public service connecting the outlying coastal villages with the great city far in land. Leaning back into the threadbare cushioning lining the interior, she looked across the narrow space to the opposite side. Maximus the town elder (Noel) smiled at her, cat-like. He wasn't just smiling at her pretty face, but other things unsaid, things she was unaware of. This ignorance only seemed to delight him further.

Beryl was still trying to wake up. "What am I doing here?"

Maximus (Noel) lent forward, as if dealing with a simpleton. "It would appear that you're travelling to the city."

She stretched back to the window, looked at the grey clouds washed across the sky. "No," she shook her head. "I can't go there. I have to get back to the village. Rufus won't know what has happened to me." She gasped. "He might think I drowned."

"It's been taken care of, dear lady," Maximus (Noel) assured her. "He knows you're alive but he doesn't want to see you."

"No..."

"It was for the best. We told him you were carrying another man's child."

"No!" She staggered up, the carriage not high enough for her. Hunched over, barely able to keep her balance, she rapped on the ceiling.

"We told him it was my child," he continued.

Beryl felt sick. "It's a lie," she told him, before throwing her head back to scream at the driver. "Let me off!"

Maximus (Noel) looked amused. "Which part?"

The carriage shuddered to a halt as Beryl was fighting with the door latch. It unhooked suddenly, swinging out and almost pulling her fully out, to topple in the dirt. Grasping the sides of the doorway, she caught her balance, lurching rather ungracefully as if about to be sick.

"When is the next carriage back to the village?"

"Not till tomorrow," the driver snapped as he heaved her trunk down from the top and flung it roughly to the heather. "Looks like you're walking." He laughed and cracked the whip, horses whinnying as they started up again, trotting away down the track. Beryl remained in the kicked dust, a wretch in crumpled skirts, her hair untied and blowing tangled in the upland winds. She had no idea how many miles from home she was.

Curling her fingers around the end handle of the trunk, she pulled it onto its side and started down the track, dragging the trunk through the mud. It jolted on her arm, tugging at the shoulder socket. It was so heavy, what had she been taking with her; a collection of sea rocks? A short way down the track, she stopped, out of breath from the exertion. She couldn't continue like this; she'd never get back to the village. Letting go of the handle, the trunk clattered heavily to the ground. She'd have to abandon it. The only thing she needed was to get back to Rufus (Adrien).

Digging her shoes into the earth, she pushed at the trunk, rolling it up off the side of the track and into the heather. At least this way it would be out of the way of the carriages, and maybe one day she'd be back to pick it up. As she ran a hand across the top, the first drops of rain, fat and heavy, splattered on the leather bound surface.

Pulling her shawl around her shoulders, she abandoned the trunk, and continued back down the track, a solitary figure in miles and miles of uninhabited moorland. The skies darkened, thick clouds blotting out the sun, and the rain began to pour, drenching the earth and all who walked upon it.

She was in a dip in the land, almost a valley. She could see the silhouette of a dead tree on the peak of a hill, its branches like gnarled fingers, illuminated by a flash of lightening. The rain thrashed on her; poured across her eyes so that she could barely see. Something pulled at her skirts, her legs, and when she looked down she realised she was wading knee-deep through marsh land, through thick sloppy mud. So viscous she could barely move. She screamed in frustration. She couldn't continue in this direction. She was going to have to get back to higher ground.

Extracting herself from the stagnant, foul-smelling bog, she scrambled up the steep slope to the top of the hill. The rain relented into a light drizzled, as she staggered, coughing, onto the stony track across moorland. She walked, her footsteps growing steadier, more determined. Up ahead, just to the side of a track, a rough rectangular stone protruded from the heather. A milestone. Picking up her skirts, she ran to the milestone. Perhaps she might be closer to home than she realised. But as she saw the engraved words on the stone, she realised that she was heading in the wrong direction. This stone only referred to the great city.

Turning 180 degrees, she started to run down the track. She lost hold of her shawl, the wind whipping it out across the moors. Beryl didn't care; she just wanted to be home. Hurrying around a sharp bend in the road, she stumbled to a halt as the track petered out into nothing, cliffs marking a steep drop to thick wooded valleys below. Careful footsteps to the edge, Beryl peered over, looking at the jagged rocks, the sheer rock face. There was no path down, and she was hardly attired for rock climbing. The rain increased in urgency. She started to cry. Why was this so complicated?

It was another dejected trudge back the way she had come. She came to crossroads she'd not seen before, a wooden signpost leaning at an awkward angle from a pile of rocks. Crossing over the tracks, she stepped up the slight embankment to try and see the signpost better. It wasn't in a language she knew.

A rumbling and a cry of a horse. A carriage rolled up to the crossroads, stopping neatly by the signpost. Beryl turned and looked up at the driver. "Where are you going?"

"To the city," he told her.

The carriage door clicked open and Maximus (Noel) leaned out. "Come inside, now," he said, offering a hand to help her back into the carriage. "We're all growing older. We can't go back."

There was a police car parked outside the hotel. It had arrived at eight o'clock that morning, and two uniformed police constables had gone into the property. Five minutes after that Huw Dodd had entered the building. That had all been ten minutes ago. Nothing more had happened, as if the scene was stuck on pause and the recording needed restarting.

Beryl was watching from a safe distance, perched on the edge of a damp sun lounger by the swimming pool. It wasn't raining today, although the clouds still littered the sky. The remains of the recent deluge were apparent everywhere. After two days hidden in the flat crying and gibbering to herself, she had finally calmed down. Taken a sober look in the bathroom mirror. She was not perfect, no one was, and as she accepted this, she could find some peace.

Today was her last full day in the village, and she'd decided to treat herself to a proper breakfast. As she'd walked towards the hotel, she'd had to step to the side of the road for a police car to drive past. She'd seen it park beside the hotel as she'd approached, and something unspoken had stopped her from entering the building. So instead she had selected her vantage point and waited.

There was the sound of voices, and some figures appeared from the hotel. The hotel manager, who at first appeared to be leading the gathering out, then moved to the side, remaining motionless, solemn. Huw Dodd emerged, followed by the police constables. A few nods, curt mumblings, then the police constables and Huw got into the car and drove away.

Had they already made the connection between Ffion and Huw? Beryl thought over what Adrien had told her. How would Huw ever convince them of a suicide, after all these years past? As much as he had never wanted it, he and Ffion were now permanently tied to one another. He'd not escape her.

Someone coughed awkwardly behind her. Beryl glanced over her shoulder, saw Noel close by, standing rather sheepishly. This was very early in the morning for Noel to be out and about. "Did you see that too?"

She nodded.

"It won't do him any harm for a little public suffering after what he did to her," Noel said calmly.

"You think it'll be a quick interview in the station and that'll be the end of it?"

"Naturally," Noel said, as if this should have been obvious. "Too little of what he deserves, but never mind. I understand the police are looking into a few missing persons cases. But he'll be able to prove she's still alive."

Of course, Beryl thought. Noel doesn't know what really happened. He thinks Ffion just walked out of North Wales and started her life somewhere else, as most people have presumed all these years. He doesn't know what really happened. What Huw's been living with all this time. "You were here, weren't you?" she asked, not bothering to turn and look at him.

"When she left? Yes, I was staying here that summer. As every summer," he added, sounding a little regretful. "I follow family tradition and squander my fortune on long meaningless stays in the village. My sister at least has been more adventurous in blowing her share. She's been all over the world now."

Beryl stood up. The air was still damp, and it was chilly just sitting.

"Beryl," Noel started awkwardly, approaching her like a naughty school boy. "I understand you're leaving us tomorrow. I wanted to make friends before you left. I was beastly the other evening, but I hope you can let bygones be bygones."

She looked over at him. His eyes were tinged with bloodshot. The great writer.

"Can I buy you breakfast?"

She shrugged. "Sure."

They left the pool area and started down towards the hotel. "What do you think happened to Ffion?"

"Ffion?" Noel looked up to the sky for inspiration. "I have no idea, but I don't think they found her in the woods. Huw treated her like crap, but he had no reason to kill her. She'll be living somewhere else, getting on with her life. I hope if she hears of this, she doesn't come forward too soon. She should make him suffer. No less than what he did to her. I saw a lot of what went on, you know. The police will quiz him, make him squirm a bit. He'll have to admit to what a bastard he is. Then I suppose he'll show them Ffion's postcards, and they'll have to let him go."

"Do you think he'd even bother with them, knowing they're fakes?"

"Fakes?"

"Well, yes, obviously. They're not in Welsh."

Noel didn't respond immediately, rather he gazed out to sea as if mesmerized by a new thought. "Welsh," he breathed to himself as if he'd just discovered the meaning of life.

Beryl slowed to a stop. "How do you know about the postcards?" She couldn't imagine that Huw would have confided such a thing to someone like Noel. He'd only just told Adrien about the cards a few months ago. Fifteen years of emotionally charged messages from around the world, all the while knowing they were fakes. Not only because they were in English, but because Ffion was dead. This was torment set up by someone else with an axe to grind.

"Oh, you know, the usual." Noel stopped and turned, looking in her direction, but not meeting her eye.

"Oh Jesus, Noel," Beryl burst out, furious with him. "It was you, wasn't it? You've been writing those bloody postcards all these years. What did you do, get your sister to post them on her travels?"

"You don't need to feel sorry for him," Noel said. "You never saw the way he treated her."

"Maybe not, but it's been fifteen years. I've seen those postcards; my god, that is some piece of work. How long do you bear a grudge?"

"That man..."

"Didn't do anything to you! Whatever went on between him and Ffion wasn't any of your business." It isn't any of your concern either, a little Adrien-toned voice inside reminded her. "What gives you the right to psychologically torture someone like that for so long?"

Noel scowled at her. "Don't be so bloody naive."

Beryl waved him off like an irritating buzzing fly. "Forget breakfast. I'm not hungry anymore."

Noel stayed and watched her march back to her flat. Silly haughty little madam. He'd had such hopes pinned on that one; they'd all been dashed. Still, she wasn't going to spoil his appetite. He wandered back to the hotel, sauntering into the restaurant area. It was quite empty, apart from a few paying guests and a skinny, curly-haired man that seemed familiar but he couldn't quite place. He walked across the room and took his usual place by the window. Glanced out at the sea front. It didn't look as though it was going to be a particularly marvellous day.

She'd admitted to breaking a glass and paid for the damage. Handed in the keys at the Castle Deudrath reception desk, and checked out of Portmeirion. Shouldering her rucksack, handbag hung over the crook of her arm, suitcase on wheels pulled behind, she slowly made her way up the road into the real village and the Minffordd mainline railway station, well in mind that she had almost an hour before the train would arrive. There was no one at the platform, just a little touch of mist. Beryl set her suitcase upright, and popped her handbag on top. Checked her coat pocket for the train tickets she'd bought online two weeks ago. It was the same journey that had brought her here, only in reverse to complete the circle.

She'd seen Cerys yesterday afternoon. A bit of a subdued goodbye, but they had parted on friendly terms, which was more than could be said for her other last exchanges with people of Portmeirion. She and Cerys had promised to keep in touch, but she didn't know how long the good intentions would last. When the connection, whether it was a place, a job or a university course, ended, it took something extra that often wasn't there to keep the contact and friendship going. Perhaps no one would want to be reminded of the last three months.

Cerys had updated her on all the news. Dafydd had found another job – somewhat pointlessly now because it looked as though Huw wouldn't be back. They still weren't sure if he was being charged with anything or just helping the police with their enquiries, but it was doubtful he would want to be in Portmeirion again after this. The body was definitely that of Ffion Owen. That much he had confirmed. Adrien had handed in his notice and would be leaving the village in a month's time. No one knew what he was planning to do, although Cerys rather suspected he'd be heading back to Italy.

It was all change for everyone concerned, new starts. All except Noel who would continue in ever decreasing circles of bitterness, and Beryl who would return to her old life in York. Nothing much to look forward to, but she'd had enough excitement for one year.

A distant rattle. Beryl stepped up to the edge of the platform and peered down the length of the tracks. The train was approaching. She returned to her luggage, pushing the suitcase handle down into the case so it would be easier to manhandle into a luggage rack. Hooked the handbag back into the crook of her arm.

The train pulled into the station, the carriage doors released with a hiss. A few day trippers for the village dismounted. Beryl waited by the side of the door, watching them, before picking up her suitcase and heaving it into the train. She found a spare slot on the ground shelf, pushing the case into place, before walking into the carriage as the train jolted and began to move again. She took a seat in an empty corner of the train, slipping into a window seat, her bags beside her. Gazed out of the window at the greenery, the scenery. Goodbye Wales.

The train rattled down the coast, swinging around to continue up the side of the estuary, inland, where it started to break apart into rivers. Stopping at Penrhyndeudraeth station, then following an arc around to cross over the wide river, the lines and the single lane road snugly together crossing on the same bridge. Then back down the estuary, the outlook of flat marshy plains and rocky mountainscapes switching sides in the carriage. Beryl was now on the side of the sea, looking across lush green sheep fields, spreading flatly out towards the sea and tidal-washed sands, the greenery of the land beyond. As the train approached the little station of Talsarnau, she got a good view across to Portmeirion. A thickly wooded, steep headland, the brightly painted buildings emerging from the branches, showing from the top of the village down the hill to the hotel by the waterside. The little zigzagged pathway from the top, punctuated by white walls and little folly towers with pan tiles.

Talsarnau was barely a village, the even smaller station lying just outside, a single raised platform on one side of the tracks. The train stopped, for it was a popular point for keen walkers and birders. From here, at the right time during the tides, people could walk out to the island in the estuary. The platform was on the other side of the train to Beryl. She stared out onto the fields; her forehead pressed to the cool glass, and sighed to herself. Listening to the movement of people getting off the train, others embarking.

The train started to move again. Footsteps moved down the carriage, stopping at her table. Thinking it was the ticket inspector, she sat up, pulling the envelope with the tickets from her jacket pocket.

But it wasn't the ticket inspector. It was Adrien. He looked particularly tired, haggard. His hair was in a disarray. And yet he could now relax. Beryl opened her mouth, utterly bewildered by his sudden appearance on the train. He was carrying a paper bag, which he lifted and set on the table. "I think you're the best person to decide what to do," he told her.

Beryl glanced at the bag, then back to Adrien. "I..."

"I'm sorry," he interrupted. "I'm sorry for how things worked out." He paused, as if not sure what to do now, then stuck out a hand in her direction. Beryl tentatively took it.

"Goodbye, Beryl."

"Goodbye, Adrien."

The train soon pulled into the next station, Tygywn, another solitary platform just before a level crossing. Adrien nodded to her before dismounting the train. This time the platform was on her side of the carriage, and she could see him from her window. He walked to the back of the platform, then turned and looked directly at her, that solemn, serious look that was so characteristic. A lurch rolled through the carriage and everything within, then the train started to move again. Beryl held up a hand, watching him grow smaller and smaller, and then he was gone.

She slipped back into her seat and looked over at the paper bag he'd left on the table. She didn't even need to look to know what was in there.

The rest of the journey was rather uneventful. The rain started again and the mists rolled down from the mountains. Beryl dozed on and off, but did not dream. Time passed quickly and the first leg of her journey home was over as the train pulled into Shrewsbury station. Last stop.

Collecting her bags, Beryl stepped out onto the platform. She had twenty minutes before the train to Manchester would arrive. Pulling her suitcase along, she went to the toilet block in the centre of the platform, struggling with the amount of luggage and the logistics of shutting the cubicle door. And when she was ready to go out, the entire pantomime was to be repeated again. Setting the paper bag to the side of the sinks, handbag still in the crook of her arm, she washed her hands. As she dried them on a paper towel, she gazed down at the paper bag, the glossy printed holiday images of the postcards on the top of the pile. Not really any of her business.

Balling up the paper towel, she threw it into the bin. Taking the suitcase handle, she left the room and the paper bag standing by the sinks.

A note on the language

The Welsh spoken in this story comes from a number of sources – none of which are my fluency in Welsh (I can but wish). For two questions asked by Cerys early on in the story, I have to thank a lovely Welsh lady from Southern Wales who translated these for me. Many thanks, Helen. The singular words are gathered online, and the antiquated line is from a medieval Welsh poem. Any mistakes are my own.

www.ingramcontent.com/pod-product-compliance
Lightning Source LLC
Chambersburg PA
CBHW051835170626
46807CB00003B/1197